T0156589

By the same author:

Hope Dies Last
In the Whirlwind of History
Blood Red Moon
Inspector Bourke in Sydney, Bangkok and Moscow
Valley of Dreams
Countess Megan of Bondi
The Gagarin Mystery
Out of Sight

THE END OF
THE WORLD

21 December 2012 – MAYA PROPHECY
Second enlarged edition

Tibor Timothy Vajda

iUniverse, Inc.
New York   Bloomington

The End of the World
21 December 2012 - Maya Prophecy

iUniverse books may be ordered through booksellers or by contacting:

iUniverse
1663 Liberty Drive
Bloomington, IN 47403
www.iuniverse.com
1-800-Authors (1-800-288-4677)

Because of the dynamic nature of the Internet, any Web addresses or links contained in this book may have changed since publication and may no longer be valid. The views expressed in this work are solely those of the author and do not necessarily reflect the views of the publisher, and the publisher hereby disclaims any responsibility for them.

ISBN: 978-1-4401-2204-0 (sc)
ISBN: 978-1-4401-2205-7 (ebook)

Printed in the United States of America

iUniverse rev. date: 2/11/2009

Grateful thanks to my wife Eva for her untiring help and Penelope Grace for her assisting in editing.

SOLSTICE JUNE 2008

It was 28ᵗʰ of February, 2008, and Mr Bert Harvey had just finished his lesson to junior students at the Chicago South Number 18 High School. The subject was Meso-American history, the history of the Incas.

The bell rang and the teacher closed the book he was reading from. Then he noticed something unusual. He looked around and realized that none of the students had jumped up and run towards the door as they usually did when they heard the bell. They stayed transfixed in their seats, staring into the distance. They look hypnotized with their mouths open, told himself Mr Harvey and started towards the door. Before leaving the class he turned around. When he saw the same scene, the seemingly hypnotized boys and girls, he called out: "That's all. Next week we will talk about the Spanish conquest of Meso-America."

Matthew Bolger walked home from school with his friend, Justin Rover, and they were discussing Mr Harvey 's lesson. Both had found it very interesting.

"I wish I could go and see that Lake Titicaca Mr Harvey was talking about. Imagine! A whole city submerged and still existing under the lake," said Matthew.

"You could see it!" Justin told him. "It's your real birthday tomorrow, isn't it, 29th February? Don't you get special privileges when it's a leap year? Ask your Mom to take you there. She does everything for you."

"You know, you're not half as dumb as you look, Justin," said Matthew jokingly. "You've given me an idea. Tomorrow is my twelfth birthday. Next year I'll be a man! Ha, ha! Mr Harvey talked about the special festivities at the solstices. Thousands of tourists flock to Lake Titicaca. There are cheap flights too. I'll ask Mom to take me there for the solstice in June. What do you reckon?"

"That's cool, man. You could go scuba diving and see those submerged cities for yourself," said Justin. "It'll be winter there then, but not very cold, I'd say."

"Righto, I'll jump Mom tonight. Pity my Dad won't be there, not even on my birthday. They're divorced and that's that. Too bad! See you tomorrow," said Matthew and with that they parted.

As soon as he got home Matthew logged onto his PC and started searching for everything about the Incas, their life, their religion and the history of the rising of the Inca Empire until the Spaniards invaded and ruined it.

When Matthew heard his mother coming, he ran down from his room in the attic without logging off and jumped into her arms, breathing fast, and began nagging her.

His mother, Sarah, got a fright. She thought something bad had happened and upset her only son.

"Mom, you know what day it is tomorrow, don't you? Leap years are special for me, aren't they?"

Sarah, who was used to Matthew's sudden outbursts, realized that the great excitement was only caused by his expectations.

"Of course I know. Just try to relax a bit and tell me what you'd like for your birthday, where should we go to celebrate?"

She thought about taking Matthew to a show and going out for dinner at a restaurant. She also wanted to find out whether he wanted to have a new baseball bat or glove. Matthew's answer caught her by surprise.

"We should go to Lake Titicaca in Peru. In leap years everyone in America takes advantage of the special holiday packages. There are festivities and dances. We could see the floating islands and the submerged cities. There'll be catamaran sight-seeing trips and scuba diving too." Matthew found it hard to keep breathing and speaking at the same time. "There's everything I always wanted to see!" he said and took a deep breath.

Sarah couldn't have been more surprised. She didn't want to hurt Matthew's feelings on his special day, so she said slowly: "You never talked about that lake before, Matthew. What's made it so interesting all of a sudden? It's on the other side of the world, you know."

"We're having lessons about the Incas now. We've never heard anything half as interesting as what Mr Harvey has told us about the Incas.

"You're worried about the money, aren't you?" asked Matthew. "Well, you don't have to worry. I've checked on the Internet, and there are special package deals for the solstice from Chicago to Peru, including accommodation in Puno, right on the shore of Lake Titicaca.

"Please, Mom, please," begged Matthew. "You told me I'll be a 'man' next year but I won't have another real birthday for four years and by then, after I finished school, I'll be studying in college or be working.

"This is my last chance. You don't have to spend any money on birthday presents, I'll be alright without pocket money too. Just let's get to see the wonderful Lake Titicaca. Please, Mom, please,"

Matthew hugged his mother tight and looked into her face with teary eyes.

"Okay, let's say I'll do my best to get away from work for a holiday, and you'll search the Internet for the cheapest travel deals... Okay?"

"Couldn't Dad help out too? It's a special occasion."

"You can forget your Dad. He's married again and they have a baby. He has enough problems. Don't even try to get him involved. I can take care of us without him."

*   *   *

WHEN THE 20ᵀᴴ OF JUNE arrived, it seemed to Matthew that his wildest dream had come true. At 8 a.m. Matthew and Mrs Bolger boarded the charter flight to Peru at the Chicago O'Hare airport and with one refuelling stop at Miami, they arrived in Peru the same evening. At the Juliaca airport the bus of the Puno hotel, Caminas de Salinas Real, was waiting for them.

The mass of people running around, the noise and Matthew's constant nagging, "Look, Mom," caused Mrs Bolger a bad headache. As soon as they settled into their hotel room she took two pain killers and lay down, asking Matthew to leave her alone for a while and keep himself busy.

The 21ˢᵗ of June was a warm, pleasant day. People were running around in bathing costumes, shouting to each other the names of the places they were going to. Matthew had a hundred suggestions but his mother just didn't have the strength to follow them on the first morning.

"It's too early. Why don't we just go on the beach? I could sit down in the shade and read a magazine. You could find the place where you rent the scuba diving gear and find out where the best spots are to see things that are submerged.

"Don't forget that you're not supposed to go scuba diving alone. It must be done in pairs. It's not without dangers. You have to find an experienced pair for yourself. You've never tried the sport before, remember."

With this Mrs Bolger let Matthew go on his discovery tour while she sat down with an American magazine to read in the shade of a beach umbrella.

Her peace and quiet lasted almost an hour. She was shaken by Matthew's loud return with a young boy. *He couldn't be more than thirteen or fourteen,* thought Mrs Bolger.

"Mom, this is Paco. His father is the owner of the boat and scuba diving gear shop. They're just a kilometre up on the shore. When I told them that I need a pair, Paco's father said his son could go with me. He is an experienced scuba diver. Renting the whole gear is just twenty American dollars. Isn't it wonderful, Mom?"

During Matthew's whole speech his mother's only thought was that the boy was too young to be trusted to take care of Matthew but seeing how enthusiastic Matthew was she knew that she had no chance of stopping him in his new adventure. "Alright, but don't go far out on the water. Stay in the area where I can see you two..."

Before Sarah finished her words Matthew cut in. "No problem. The lake is not very deep here and the ruins are not more than about 200 metres from the shore. Am I right, Paco?"

Paco nodded enthusiastically but judging by his facial expression Mrs Bolger had the impression that he didn't understand English very well.

Despite all warnings of his mother that scuba diving is dangerous, Matthew, who had never tried the sport before, swam far away from the boat, away from his mother's and Paco's watching eyes.

He swam deeper and deeper, lost contact with the boat and soon lost consciousness in the lake.

Matthew was woken from his slumber by water rushing on his face. *Am I in a shower?* he asked himself before opening his eyes.

It was a strange sensation. He felt like the astronaut trainees must have felt in an airless chamber. He saw them on television moving grotesquely, 'swimming' inside the airless cabin. Where am I? He looked around.

What he saw amazed him.

An unknown force propelled him along a tunnel with great speed. The tunnel had no walls. The rushing air seemed to produce the tunnel as it passed under water and sometimes under land, pushing fish, and other marine animals aside. From time to time sunrays shone through the top of the tunnel. That made Matthew think *I mustn't be too deep in the water.*

How long will my air last? Matthew turned to check the compressed air cylinder on his back. There was no cylinder. Matthew got scared. *I have no air, how can I breathe?*

Matthew tried to move his arms and legs and he had no problem with that. However, when he tried to turn back and move backwards, he couldn't. The force kept propelling him forwards, regardless of his efforts, against his will. He realized that he was able to breathe under water, without any air supply.

I'm breathing like a fish! said Matthew to himself. *Some force is carrying me off to some destination, but for what possible purpose? What would Mom think happened? What would she do?*

Realizing that his speculations were useless and he was unable to do anything, Matthew closed his eyes, tried to relax and let the 'force' carry him along wherever it intended to take him.

WHEN THE RUSH STOPPED MATTHEW opened his eyes. He was standing on the banks of a great lake. It was in the tropics, with palms, coconut trees and lush shrubs all around.

Where am I? What am I doing in this strange place? Are there any people here? While Matthew was wondering about his situation a tall man approached from the distance. As he came closer, Matthew saw he was wearing the type of toga and sandals the Roman senators used to wear 2000 years ago. Matthew had seen drawings of them in his textbooks on Roman history.

To Matthew's great surprise the man called out to him in English.

"You are Matthew from Lake Titicaca, aren't you?"

"Yes, I am," answered Matthew who couldn't stop himself asking: "How come you speak English?"

"Oh, that's not a problem here in Paititi. You will have a small insert in your head as we all have, a sort of microchip, containing software for automatic translation of all languages. Language is not a problem here at all," said the man with a reassuring smile.

"By the way, my name is Virgil, you may have heard about me. I will be your guide, but first we have to wait for your brothers. They should be here soon."

"You are mistaken, I have no brothers," said Matthew. Just as soon as he said that, however, two young men who seemed to be the same age as him walked up the shore. One of them was a blond, white-skinned boy, the other completely the opposite. He was black and had curly black hair.

"You are Oleg from Siberia and you are Patrice from Africa. Right? Welcome to you all in Paradise," Virgil greeted them with a bow.

"First of all I'll take you to the hospital to fix your language problems. With this Virgil took the boys to a small, white building where they had to lie down and were given a drink. The liquid had a strong spicy taste and smelled of alcohol. The boys first hesitated to drink it but at Virgil's encouraging smile they drank it. The liquid was a powerful anaesthetic which kept them unconscious while the surgeon inserted a tiny microchip into their brain.

In a short while the boys regained consciousness and were able to get up. First timidly, then freely, they started to talk. Soon they realized that they understood each other's language though Oleg spoke in Russian, Patrice in Swazi and Matthew in English.

They soon found out that they had corresponding histories and guessed that was the reason for their abduction. They were all 'leaplings' and had just had their twelfth birthday. They had been abducted on the day of the June solstice: Matthew in Peru from Lake Titicaca, Patrice in Africa from Lake Challa, on Mount Kilimanjaro, and Oleg in Siberia from Lake Bajkal.

"Where are we and what is going to happen to us?" asked the boys in unison.

"Virgil told me we were brought here for the summer solstice festivities which they celebrate on the 24th of June and not on the 21st as we do in the U.S.," said Matthew, though he couldn't remember Virgil actually telling him that. *What was this? Hhypnosis? Telepathy?*

Virgil returned and told the boys to sit down in front of him.

"Of course, you would like to know why you were brought here. I can tell you that you are going to have a glorious experience in Agartha, as we call the Middle Earth where we are living, in the middle of the hollow Earth.

"They mislead you when they teach you that the Earth is a solid ball. Far from it. Three worlds exist on our planet. The Outer Surface, the Middle Earth which contains natural and man-made caverns and tunnels, and then there's the Inner Surface.

"The inner sun, Atoma, provides the Middle Earth with 24 hour sunlight every day. There are land masses and bodies of water in

Middle Earth and in the Inner Earth, the same as on the Outer Surface.

"Millions of years ago, when the ancient super continent, Pangea, broke into Lemuria and Gondwanaland, the people from the northern part, Lemuria, occupied Middle Earth. They are by now much more developed in many ways than the ones living on the Outer Surface.

"We have spacecraft that are not affected by gravity. They lift up through the hole at the northern polar region.

"From time to time we check on what people on the Outer Surface are doing.

"At the last winter solstice Inti, the Sun God, ordered his son, called The Inca, to bring three leaplings at the dawn of their manhood and sacrifice them to ensure good results in all their endeavours for the following year. Initiation into manhood on the Outer Surface is at the age of thirteen but here it is at fourteen. This gives us more opportunity to prepare them for their glorious duties."

"What will be our duties, Virgil?" asked Oleg.

"You were chosen for the extreme sacrifice, the most honourable duty. The most capable of you will be sacrificed first, to the Sun God, by the High Priest. The other two will be sacrificed one after the other in the following years.

"But that's enough of that," said Virgil when he saw how the boys' faces went white hearing that they were to be sacrificed. "I am taking you to your new quarters and will present you to the Son of the Sun King."

Virgil led the boys through a large garden, full of palms, fruit-bearing trees and a great variety of plants and flowers. There were pools too. Virgil remarked that the pools were for baptismal rituals.

From the garden, a wide avenue led into a huge building. There were pink marble sculptures of mythical animals along both sides of the avenue. Rows of giant columns led into a hall that was so long one could not see its full length.

A few men were standing between the columns and they wore garments made from blue sheets. A hole had been cut for their heads and the sides were kept together with large pins.

The ceiling of the enormous hall mirrored the night sky with stars. The huge scale of everything created a majestic scene. There was a square enclosure in the middle of the hall. "That is the Temenos, the sacred place for the worshippers," said Virgil.

The boys recognized the colourful carved and painted foliage on the capitals of the pillars. They represented tropical vegetation, lotuses and palm trees.

At the end of the hall there was a smaller room, carved into the hill. There were stone carvings on the lintels. The Inca sat there on a golden throne.

Though The Inca was sitting, the boys could see that he was a muscular, strongly built man. His straight black hair reached his shoulders. His dark-red cloak had a high collar. The sleeves were decorated by vertical black, blue and gold stripes. The Inca's light bronze-coloured face was impassioned when he spoke. His speech showed a man used to giving orders.

Virgil led the three boys to The Inca, bowing deeply, and introduced them by their names and their country of origin.

"You're most welcome here and we have given you Virgil, the best teacher we have, to help you with your studies and with your transformation," said The Inca and, with a gesture of his right hand, dismissed them.

Virgil ushered them to the side and told them, "We are staying to see the wedding ceremony."

There were two huge gold pillars on each side of The Inca's throne. Each was covered by letters and drawings from the ground to their top.

Answering Oleg's question, Virgil said that the strange writing on the gold pillars contained the full description of the history of Middle Earth.

"In what language is the history written?" asked Patrice.

"It is in Aramaic, the ancient sacred language," Virgil told him.

"And what language is spoken by people of the Middle Earth today?" asked Matthew. "Quechua," Virgil told him.

While the boys were looking around to absorb the strange surroundings, they heard loud applause and saw a tall, strongly built man standing in front of The Inca. He kept applauding. "He is the High Priest, the Villac Uma," Virgil told them.

From two sides of the colonnades boys and girls appeared. The boys stood on the right side of the High Priest, in a line facing him, the girls made a parallel line on his left. Matthew guessed the young people in both lines were about 18 years old. The girls wore long, red skirts. From their knees down the skirts had colourful embroideries depicting pictures of trees, valleys, mountains. They wore golden leather sandals. Each girl had a pearl headband with a star of topaz on her forehead.

When the High Priest applauded again the first boy walked over to the line of the girls and without saying a word led a girl by her arm and returned to his original place, placing the girl behind him. On further applause by the High Priest one by one the boys selected their partners and stood them behind themselves.

The actual marriage ceremony was very short. The Inca spoke for a few minutes about the duties of the husbands and wives towards Him and towards the state, then the High Priest jangled bells, blew a horn and danced a few steps. With extended arms and open hands he blessed them in the name of Inti, the Sun God, and the ceremony was over.

After the marriage ceremony was over, everybody left the hall with the exception of a few worshippers. Virgil led the boys to one of the side rooms and told them that it was now theirs and he would be moving in with them too. He left and returned later with fruit and other food.

"We'll start the teaching tomorrow morning," said Virgil. "In the afternoon and in the evening we'll take part in the summer solstice festival. It will be magnificent, you will see," he promised them. The boys didn't mind the delay in their indoctrination; they waited excitedly to see the promised spectacles.

The summer solstice festival was indeed breathtaking. Not far from the Sacred Hall, six storeys of terraces were cut into a hill. They were connected by sliding ramparts. People stood side by side, completely filling the terraces, singing the praise of Inti Raymi with their right arms raised toward heaven.

"It is the eternal consecration of the tie between the Sun and his children, the human beings," Virgil told them.

On every terrace the people wore sheeting garments of different colours, worn in toga fashion. Blue, red and yellow dominated the scene.

There was a bonfire in the middle of the main square. People were chanting, singing and dancing ecstatically to the beating of drums around the bonfire.

This kept the boys up late and the next morning Virgil started their teaching.

"The Golden Rules of the Empire of the Sun were: do not steal, do not be idle, and do not lie. These rules have not changed since the dawn of time," Virgil told them.

"Time, in the Empire of the Sun, is measured by cosmic cycles. A one thousand year cycle was called an *inti*, which meant the Sun. The thousand year cycles were divided into halves and each half was called a *pachakuti*. The transitional times between the *pachakutis* were characterized by great changes.

"During the eighth *pachakuti* everything flourished. It was the time of the Light. The ninth *pachakuti* brought five hundred years of the Dark. That was when the Spanish invaders destroyed the Inca Empire.

"We are now entering the tenth *pachakuti*, the return of the Light. This is the time when the cities of the Fourth Dimension, the lost golden cities and the ethereal city under Lake Titicaca, will flourish again.

"According to legend, at the time when Lemuria was sinking and became the Middle Earth, one of the seven great masters of Lemuria, Lord Aramu Meru, brought the sacred Golden Solar Disc from the Temple of Illumination to Lake Titicaca for safe keeping. He placed it in the Ethereal City under the lake.

"The Solar Disc was used in the capacity of a Cosmic Computer that received information directly from the Universal Mind Source at the centre of the Galaxy. By opening themselves spiritually, The Inca and the High Priest can access the cosmic wisdom. It is during this time, the time of the tenth *pachakuti*, when the Solar Disc is to be reactivated to access the cosmic wisdom. The Sun Gates in the lakes from which you were abducted are portals through which new energies are entering Mother Earth."

"Does the release of new energies mean there'll be sacrifices?" asked Matthew. "Yes," answered Virgil. Complete silence followed. *Which one of us will be the first?* wondered the three.

The days and months passed fast, and the three guests learned a lot from Virgil, but the three young men could never chase away the question; which one of them will be sacrificed next December, at the summer solstice celebration.

They learned that about 225 million years ago there was only one continent on the globe called Pangea. About 200 million years ago the super continent broke in two. The Northern part became Laurasia, while the Southern part became Gondwanaland. From about 150 million years on, gradually the present five continents have emerged as a result of continuous movements of the tectonic plates that cover the globe.

Matthew interrupted the lecture with:

"We have learned so much from you, Virgil, but you've never told us about the way we got transported here. It's true, we never asked, but please, tell us.."

"Alright, I'll tell you the essence of it. Try to understand," said Virgil.

"We have learned from the Cosmic Computer that "Thoughts have an energy that attracts energy. In order to control this energy one has to practice four things:

"First, know what one desires and ask the Universe for it. (By the Universe one could mean God, or an unknown source of energy.)

"Second, focus one's thoughts upon the thing desired with great feeling, such as enthusiasm or gratitude.

"Third, feel and behave as if the object of one's desire has already obtained.

"Fourth, finally, be open to receive it."

The boys kept quiet and looked confused when Virgil asked them whether they understood him.

"How does this work in practice?" asked Matthew.

Vigil gave an example:

"The Inca and the High Priest closet themselves together and for 24 hours they concentrate on the desired thing or event.

"Take your time and think about it. If you have faith, you'll understand."

Finally they learned what interested them most: how Middle Earth, particularly Paititi, developed.

Paititi is under the former Krakatau volcano. It is in the caldera of Krakatau. The largest and most explosive volcanic eruption ejected hundreds of cubic kilometres of magma onto the Earth's surface.

When such a large volume of magma is removed from beneath the volcano, the ground subsides or collapses. A huge depression, called a Caldera, forms in the emptied space. Some calderas are more than 25 km in diameter and several kilometers deep. Man-made tunnels bridge the calderas on different continents. Basically that's the short description of how the 'Kingdom of the Sun' exists.

Two days before the summer solstice festival Virgil said goodbye to the three boys and told them that they would not meet anymore.

"Your fate will be in the hands of The Inca and the High Priest." With these words Virgil led them into a dark room behind The Inca's throne which they hadn't seen before.

The boys were clad in tunics like the ones the officials wore. The tunics were made of the finest Vicuna weavings. They were patterned with white/black checkerboard motifs, mixed with red triangles. The boys' hair was braided and various coloured cords were wrapped around their heads.

The High Priest visited them twice a day and taught them prayers and songs. They were not given food, only a cup of a thick, spicy liquid three times a day.

"Your insides have to be cleansed for the ceremony," the High Priest told them.

The boys felt dizzy all the time and gradually stopped talking to each other, only repeating the prayers and the songs they were taught.

On the day of the 22nd of December, the first day of the year in the Inca calendar, when the potato and corn harvests were finished, the boys were led up the thirty steps of the flat-topped pyramid opposite The Inca's palace.

There was a large flat block of marble in the geometric middle on top of the pyramid. The High Priest stationed Oleg on one side of the marble table and Patrice on the other side.

"This is your moment of glory," said the priest to Matthew as he laid him on the altar. He raised his arms and called to Inti, asking him to receive this sacrifice with grace.

He then raised his right arm high, holding a sharp, shiny gold knife in his hand. When the rays of the midday sun shone on the point of the knife, with one fast blow, he struck down on Matthew.

--.--.--

FOR A WHILE MRS BOLGER sat in the shade on the beach, following the scuba-diving group with her eyes as they disappeared in the distance, then she looked around. What's all that noise about? she wondered.

Tourists were crowding around local vendors who displayed their wares on the ground and from time to time said a few Spanish words to the would-be buyers – mostly American tourists – who tried to bargain loudly and forcefully.

A boat came into sight. She recognized Matthew with a number of other men in the boat.

Matthew was waving his arms and shouted, "Mom! You can see us, just watch the boat." With this Matthew turned around, pulled down the scuba diving mask on his face and jumped into the water.

As soon as Matthew disappeared into the water, one man rowed the boat Kenu-style away from the shore. Soon the boat became a small point on the horizon.

Matthew dove a couple of metres down in the lake but saw no ruins, only dark shapes which got larger as he swam downwards. The small compressed air tank felt uncomfortable on his back. *It doesn't matter it's only for a short while,* he told himself and kicked harder with his fins, completely forgetting that he was not supposed to swim too far away from the boat.

Matthew's breathing became more laborious, and he was considering turning back when he saw something that changed his mind. Further away, on the bottom, he saw the outline of a wall and a large opening, perhaps a door, or a gate? *I've found it!* enthused Matthew and swam towards the mysterious wall and the opening.

As Matthew got closer, he saw the water swirling in front of the opening in the wall. *Maybe there is a large fish there. I'll have a look before I return.* That was his last conscious thought.

About an hour has passed when Mrs Bolger realized that she hadn't seen Matthew or the boat for a while.

She jumped up and ran to the boatman on the pier asking if he'd seen Matthew and the scuba-diving group. The man said something in Spanish and turned away.

"You don't understand. My son has disappeared. Who can look for him? He was in a boat just like yours."

Only half turning back the man repeated what he'd said before and walked away.

Who is responsible here for the security of the tourists? wondered Sarah.

"We are Americans. I will report you to the American Consul and to the police," Sarah said to the back of the man as he left.

Matthew is in danger. Maybe he was kidnapped, went through her mind. "Where are the police?" she asked loudly.

A young, apparently local man in swimming shorts passed. "The police are that way," he said, pointing in the direction of a group of tourists. "By the way," he told her, "if someone falls into the lake, like a drowning fisherman, it is traditional not to rescue them but to let them drown as an offering to the Earth Goddess Pachamama." Sarah Bolger stared at the back of the young man as he walked away too. She didn't want to believe what she'd just been told.

She ran in the direction she was shown. Within minutes she saw a ramshackle timber shack with 'Hernando's Boatshed' painted on its side.

A middle aged Indian was discussing the prices of hiring equipment with customers.

"Where are the scuba-divers?" Sarah demanded.

"My son went out with your boat. About two hours ago. Where are they?"

"They are not back yet but my son is an experienced instructor. He'll bring the boat back with your son," said the man without any sign of excitement and turned to scan the horizon.

It seems that he is worried too, after all, Sarah told herself.

Minutes later the catamaran ferry that plied the lake between Puno and Puerto Acosta on the Bolivian side approached the shore.

"The ferry is flying a red flag. That means they want an ambulance to meet them at the pier," the man told Sarah who felt a stab in her heart and sat down on a used tyre lying on the beach.

Matthew, Matthew, what's happened to you? she asked herself sighing deeply. *We shouldn't have come to this cursed place,* she thought.

A man in a blue shirt, wearing a 'Policia' armband came to the pier before the ferry arrived.

Sarah immediately grabbed his arm and told him as fast as she could that her son, Matthew Bolger, an American citizen disappeared two hours ago in the lake.

The man understood and in broken English told her that the ferry had asked for an ambulance to meet it at the pier and maybe they had her son on board.

The ferry arrived, then the ambulance.

Soon two sailors appeared carrying a seemingly unconscious Matthew on a stretcher and hurried toward the waiting ambulance.

They pushed the stretcher inside the vehicle and Sarah jumped in too. They drove away fast.

The white-clad ambulance man attached an oxygen mask to Matthew's face and strapped his body to the fixed bed.

"What happened to my son?" asked Sarah. "Is he going to be alright? Is there an American hospital here with American doctors?"

The man answered in good English. "Try to relax, lady. He was taken ashore in a hyperbaric chamber after he was found unconscious among the reefs of the floating Sun Island. This is the only hyperbaric chamber in the whole district. It delivers oxygen with elevated pressure. Your son was very lucky to get this treatment."

"He is still unconscious. What is going to happen to him?"

"We take him to the Emergency Department in the Clinic Geral, the best in the district. You can go in with him and speak to the doctors after he's admitted."

"A local man told me, if I understood him correctly, that they don't usually search for people who get into difficulties in the lake. Are they all mad around here?"

"They are not mad, they are religious. Sacrifices to the Sun God, like a fisherman drowning in the lake, is a religious tradition since Inca times."

In the Emergency Department of the Policlinica Geral in Puno, Dr Emilio Castillo explained to Sarah what had happened to Matthew in Lake Titicaca.

"He was scuba diving. After a while, when he failed to return, Paco started to look for him without any success. He was afraid to return to his father without the American and just waited in the boat, when the ferry catamaran came their way.

"Paco saw that the catamaran was stationary and reversed to the floating Sun Island. They seemed to be lifting something into the boat and continuing towards the shore. Paco was sure they had found Matthew. He rowed back to Hernando.

"The guard on the ferry had seen a body in the island's reef and reported it to the captain. The captain ordered the boat to stop and lift the body aboard.

"It so happened they were delivering a new hyperbaric chamber for the Puno hospital and the adventurous captain thought to try it out. *Maybe that body still has some life in it,* he thought. This is how your son got back to you with extreme good luck or with the help of the Sun God. For a while we will keep him here on a ventilator and feed him intravenously. We will see how that goes."

"Couldn't he be transferred to the States?"

"It would be dangerous in his present state. Let's wait four days or so. You could bring an American specialist here. We'll do our best in the meantime, you can be sure of that."

Sarah went looking for accommodation close to the hospital then rang a friend in Chicago and asked her to get a specialist to come and see Matthew.

The following day her friend called back. "Professor Kenneth Custer, at the North-Western Memorial Hospital is the leading coma specialist here and he has agreed to take on Matthew's case. He could send his associate to Puno on a private plane and have Matthew brought back to the Intensive Care department of his hospital, where he would care for him himself, that is, if you can afford the expected high costs of the treatment."

Sarah had already phoned her ex-husband and after she explained him what had happened to Matthew, he agreed to share the costs with her.

Professor Custer's associate, Dr Ronald Cullen, arrived and went to see Matthew without delay.

His first question was whether the hospital had EEG (electroencephalogram) and SEM (scanning electron microscope) machines to examine Matthew. Dr Castillo proudly told him they had both machines.

After examining Matthew, Dr Cullen's diagnosis was that he had a tumour on his brain stem, and it looked inoperable. He was in a coma because his brain wasn't getting enough oxygen. The tumour was pressing on an important blood vessel.

"He has to have complete rest, be on a ventilator to help his breathing and be fed intravenously for four days. If his condition doesn't get worse, after four days we could fly him on the specially equipped private plane to Chicago and Professor Custer could take on his treatment."

"Are you sure of your diagnosis, Dr Cullen? Matthew had no symptoms at all."

"It is unusual to have this type of brain tumour in a young person but when that happens the onset can be rapid."

"Is this the only way, Doctor? Can you guarantee success?"

"Nothing is guaranteed, Madam, but this is the only thing we can do," said Dr Cullen.

Two months later Matthew Bolger was still lying in a coma at the Intensive Care Department of the North-Western Memorial Hospital. He was still on a ventilator and was being fed intravenously. His mother spent hours every day in his room talking to him, stroking his hands, watching in vain for any sign of recovery. A few times she thought she heard Matthew whisper the name, 'Virgil'.

Then Professor Custer came to Sarah with a proposal: having studied the results of his research into the new Gamma Knife Ray surgical procedures, he considered Matthew a suitable patient to use this method to remove the tumour causing his coma. Gamma Knife Ray surgery is done without knives, enabling an improved recovery rate. The Bolgers agreed to the procedure.

--.--.—

MATTHEW FELT AN ELECTRIC SHOCK in his head and opened his eyes.

He lay on the operating table in front of Professor Custer in Chicago and the surgery was just concluded. After another two weeks clinical observations he was allowed to go home where normal functions gradually returned to him.

Remarkably, he continued to be fascinated by Meso-American history with the Hollow Earth theory and the Inca history..

PART I.

---

21 December 2012

Maya Prophecy

INTRODUCTION:

YEAR 2012 AND THE GREAT Shift.

The Year 2012 is often mentioned in relation to the fact that the ancient Mayan calendar is due to end on 21st December 2012. According to Mayan elders, it marks the end of an old era and the beginning of a new one. Astrologically, it also coincides with the transition to the Age of Aquarius from the Age of Pisces. 2012 will also see a very rare alignment between the Sun, Earth and the centre of the Milky Way. (Once every 26,625 years.)

Many channelings have also pointed to this time being the marker for the great shift of transition to take place. However, the shift is generally described to take place over a time period that began in the last century and the year 2012 is when the effects will be more fully felt. The transition is about a transformation of the old energy to the new, also known as the ascension of humanity from the 3rd to the 4th dimension.

This period of time is also known as the entry of Earth into the photon belt, a belt of very high vibrational energy that is supposed to help raise the vibrations of Earth and all life forms on it, hence enabling us to make the transition to a higher dimension.

Another common viewpoint is that our DNA consists of certain 'codes' that will be activated to transform the human being in a quantum leap into one who is again aware of his own divinity – one who is connected to All There Is.

Preparing Ourselves for the Great Shift, Russel Boulding.

Various lines of evidence suggest that the Great Shift coincides with the ending of a 26,000 year cycle. This 26,000 year cycle, related to the procession of the solstices/equinoxes arising from the tilt in the Earth's axis of rotation, is recognized in the Mayan calendar and the Hindu Vedic tradition.

It is generally agreed that the year 2012 is a marker rather than a fixed and specific timeframe. The time of the shift is determined by the state of the mass consciousness, and it could happen earlier or later. Most, however, would agree that we are already in the process of the shift. The recent earth changes have very much to do with the cleansing by Mother Earth of the old energies and preparing for the new.

Cosmic Lighthouse Metaphysics Magazine.

CHAPTER ONE

It was Tuesday, the 28ᵗᴴ of February 2012 and Mr Bert Harvey has just finished giving his history lesson to the senior students in the Chicago South High School. It was cold outside and Mr Harvey, perhaps subconsciously, tried to warm up his students by telling them interesting facts related to his subject, The Incas.

"Your Spring break will start tomorrow, which is the 29ᵗʰ of February, by the way. You'll have four weeks to yourselves. Use this time to review the important facts you learned last year. Concentrate on your favourite topics – say, The Incas – and next year you could major in it. Perhaps you could then go on to College to become a historian, or an archaeologist. You could make a worse choice, believe me.

"Two things before I leave you to your own devices. One: there is an exhibition in the Field Museum of Chicago. Take your student card with you. It is free for teachers and students. The famous Mitchell-Hedges Crystal Skull is being exhibited there for a few days. It is the best known of the legendary thirteen Crystal Skulls. Only eight of them have been discovered so far, but together they are supposed to contain all the data on the birth of the Solar System and the secrets of all the sciences, like a celestial computer.

"But that's not all. One researcher at the Hewlett-Packard Research Institute reported hearing voices, complete words actually, while he worked with the Skull."

"Yeah, and pigs can fly too," said Justin Rover under his breath to his friend, Matthew Bolger, in the seat beside him.

"Most of the recovered Crystal Skulls were used to heal illness, including brain tumours, and it is recorded that they were able to change their position without human help," continued Mr Harvey .

"They react to colours and various sounds when these are directed straight at them.

"This is probably the only chance you'll ever get to experience something paranormal. Don't miss it.

"If you are willing to sacrifice another half an hour of your free time now, I can tell you about something very interesting."

"Yes, sir, please," was the loud unanimous answer.

"In November 1996, a small group of Q'eros with the leading Shaman, Don Antonio Morales, and tribal leaders visited several cities in the United States. In New York they performed a private ceremony at the cathedral of St. John the Divine. I know, because I was there myself.

"By now eight Crystal Skulls have been certified by crystallographers as being of ancient origin. There are dozens of fakes, mostly made in Germany in the last 150 years. Of course the fake Skulls have no magic power: they cannot cure illness and won't be able to prevent the end of this world, which is supposed to happen on 21st of December this year, as prophesied by the Mayans. Only all of the 13 original Crystal Skulls together can do that.

"As for those who'd ask why they should study now, when next December this world will crumble anyway, I wish to make it clear that the prophecy does not speak about the physical destruction of humanity, or the demise of all living things. The prophecy refers to the end of time 'as we know it' - the death of a way of thinking and a new way of relating to Nature and the Earth.

"In the coming years the Incas expect us to emerge into a golden age, a golden millennium of peace. The next *pachacuti* – meaning 'great change' in Quecha, the Inca language - has already begun, and it promises the emergence of a new Human Being, after the turmoil of the last five hundred years.

"We'll be able to speak more about the Incas and the Mayans next year. Off you go now, and have a good vacation. And see the Crystal Skull, it's a unique opportunity."

Matthew was definitely interested to hear everything about the Incas but now he was preoccupied with the new cell phone he had received early from his mother for his birthday the next day, the 29th of February.

The phone had a navigational map, of course showing Matthew how to get to anywhere his heart desired. While Mr Harvey searched in his briefcase for the notes he wanted to share with his students, Matthew took out his phone and turned it on for no particular reason except to see the shiny keyboard and the map. He was surprised when it suddenly started playing some music. Then he remembered he'd set the alarm to ring at midday, to try it out. Quickly he turned the alarm off and looked sheepishly around to see if he had caused a major disturbance.

"What was that music?" asked Justin.

"You know that old Peruvian song, '*El Condor Pasa?*"

"Never heard of it," said Justin, upsetting his friend.

"I remember you singing it," answered Matthew. "You know...

> *I'd rather be a sparrow than a snail,*
> *I'd rather be a hammer than a nail.*"

"Never heard of it," repeated Justin.

"Forget it. Let's hear what Mr Harvey has to say."

On Matthew's birthday the next day the two friends went to the Chicago Field Museum. To their surprise they had to queue for an hour until they got in the door. In another half an hour they were pushed into the room marked "The Mitchell-Hedges Exhibition".

In he middle of the room, on a red velvet-covered pedestal, in a large glass box, there was the object they had come to see. Two uniformed guards were standing on either side.

"I've never seen special guards for any exhibition yet," said Matthew.

The Skull was made of translucent crystal. It was life-size and it seemed anatomically correct. It even had a detachable mandible. A placard on to the front of the pedestal stated: "The Mitchell-Hedges Crystal Skull was found by the late Anna Mitchell-Hedges, a Canadian citizen, in 1924, in the ancient Mayan ruins in Lubantuun, Belize. It weighs 11.7 pounds, five inches wide, seven inches long."

The guards were urging people to move, not to stand long in front of the exhibit, yet everybody tried to hang back, if even for a minute. Matthew was no exception. He was just about to move on when the song '*El Condor Pasa*' sounded quite loudly.

Everybody looked around to find out where it came from. It took Matthew a few seconds to realize that his new phone was the culprit. He took it out of his pocket to turn off the alarm, and the bright blue light coming from the screen fell on the Skull. Matthew went stiff. He couldn't move or speak, just looked with his mouth open at the graceful girl figure that appeared inside the Skull.

"Move," Justin told him as he was being pushed by people behind him.

"Can't you see her?" asked Matthew in a trembling voice. He turned back from Justin and could still see the girl. Her gestures seemed to say something to him. *Did she want me to come back?*

wondered Matthew who was by then pushed away and couldn't see the Skull, or the girl anymore.

"Why did your phone ring, Matt?"

"It was just the alarm. I forgot it was still set to ring at midday."

As soon as they were outside the Field Museum, Matthew grabbed his friend by the collar and blasted him with:

"Did you see the girl in the Skull?"

"What girl? There was so much pushing and shoving I could hardly take a good look at the Skull. Are you nuts? What did you see, for heaven's sake?"

"Just after the alarm rang a girl appeared inside the Skull. I can't believe you didn't see her. She seemed to want to tell me something I couldn't understand, but her gestures and face showed it was important. I'll go and see her again tomorrow. Are you coming with me?"

"No way. I have baseball practice tomorrow. I want to get into shape during these four weeks, for the championship. You go if you have nothing better to do." With this the friends parted.

Matthew was sure he saw a girl in the Skull but after some time he started to doubt his own sanity. However, he decided he was not going to forget what he saw. He had to check out his experience again. But how? Justin was not going to come with him, and he definitely had to have a witness. Who else could he ask to come with him to the exhibition? Mr Harvey, that's who!

He made up his mind to tell Mr Harvey that his planned second visit to see the Crystal Skull was particularly about his 'vision'. He believed his teacher would come with him and would not ridicule him for thinking that he saw a girl in the Skull.

Early in the evening, while his mother was preparing dinner, Matthew phoned his teacher and asked to see him at his place about an interesting matter connected with the Incas. He was told to come at 11.30 a.m. next day.

In the morning, after telling his mother that he was going to baseball practice, he left in a hurry. On his way to Mr Harvey's, Matthew became more and more excited about the upcoming conversation .

CHAPTER TWO

Mr Harvey opened the door of his ground floor apartment and invited Matthew to come in and sit down in the hall while he went to bring cool lemon drinks.

"Well, tell me what you want to discuss about the Incas," his teacher said, cutting to the chase.

"You don't have to hurry, I'm alone. As you know, I'm a widower living with my only daughter Hannah. She went to gymnastics practice. Go on, talk."

"Yesterday afternoon my friend Justin and I went to see the Crystal Skull exhibition as you suggested."

"Were there many visitors? The promotion wasn't very good."

"Oh, yes. There were thousands of people who wanted to see the Crystal Skull and judging by their faces and the remarks we heard, there could be a lot more people interested in the Incas than we thought."

"What did you and Justin think?"

"Well, that's just it. Justin and I didn't see the same thing. I came to you, because I trust you. Could you to treat this conversation as confidential, like a doctor or a lawyer would, please?"

"Go on. You can trust me," said Mr Harvey. He sipped his lemon drink and leaned back on the sofa, eagerly expecting Matthew's words.

That moment the doorbell rang. "Who could that be? Excuse me for a moment," his teacher said and went to open the door. It was Hannah, Mr Harvey's sixteen-year-old daughter, in blue shorts and a skimpy white top. "They're painting the gymnasium, we couldn't practice," said Hannah as she stepped into the room.

"You two have met, I assume?" said her father. The two young ones nodded and Hannah said, "We met in the Chess Club".

Matthew looked around uncertainly, wondering what was going to happen with the confidential conversation he came to have with Hannah's father.

He saved the day by saying, "Listen, Matthew, Hannah is very much interested in the Incas too and she can keep her mouth shut, can't you dear? So let's hear your news."

Matthew thought he had no choice but to agree to the change. He was under pressure. The exhibition was closing down in three days. He wanted to visit the Crystal Skull with Mr Harvey before the Skull left Chicago.

"You told us that the Skull could move and speak under certain conditions. I think you said that these things happen rarely but perhaps light and sound might start them off."

"That's right," confirmed Mr Harvey, and sipped his drink.

"Well, to be honest, we didn't believe you. Maybe it's not right to say we didn't believe you, but we just couldn't imagine those things happening. Yesterday everything changed for me."

After saying that, Matthew stopped talking and sighed deeply. Hannah and her father looked at him with wide open eyes, expecting to hear what happened to Matthew that affected him so deeply.

"I saw a girl inside the Skull. She waved to me and I thought she asked me to come back. I asked Justin if he saw the girl too but he said he didn't. Maybe I'm going out of mind," said Matthew and sighed. "Would you come with me to see if there is really a person inside the Skull?"

"You did the right thing telling me what happened and I will certainly help you to check it out. Maybe Hannah should come with us too to have another witness. She not only knows everything I taught you, she can also speak Quecha. Let me ask you a few questions.

"Did anybody else in front of the Skull show any sign of experiencing something unusual?"

"No, not at all."

"How long did you stand in front of the Skull?"

"Twenty to 30 seconds."

"Did you hear any music, or see a colour passing through the Skull before you noticed the girl?"

"No," said Matthew quickly, then corrected himself. "Maybe… I just didn't think it significant at the time. I didn't think it was connected with what I saw."

"What was it? Think hard," Mr Harvey warned him.

Matthew took out his cell phone and just at that moment the alarm went off. Loud music filled the room and bright blue light shone out from the screen of the phone.

"*El Condor Pasa…*" said Hannah and started to sing in a language Matthew didn't understand.

"Is that what had happened in the museum? Your phone sprang into action in front of the Skull? If I remember correctly you are a leapling, aren't you? Well, your secret is solved. You are the key to the appearance of the girl in the Skull. I may have told you that the Incas were especially sensitive to certain colours, certain melodies, to leaplings and to solstices."

"Do you think that just by chance the *El Condor Pasa* and the blue colour were clues to the appearance of the girl, Mr Harvey ?"

"I am absolutely certain they were and the fact that you are a leapling may have given additional help."

"What are we going to do now?" asked Matthew.

"Well, Hannah could tell you how many hours and months I have spent in front of the computer, trying to guess the right colour and music combination to contact those in the fourth dimension, those wonderful Incas. Now it has happened by chance, or with the help of God, the Force, maybe even the Sun-God. It doesn't matter who or what, it only matters that we are on the threshold of solving the great secret. By the way I am a leapling too. Now we have to be very careful when we plan our next steps. We are a team. Am I right, Matthew?"

"Yes, sir, you can certainly count on me," answered Matthew enthusiastically.

"By he way, I saw the Skull too yesterday," continued Mr Harvey, "and recognised one of the two security guards. He was Tony Vukic, my former student, who quit school before matriculating. He was a good sportsman and had a good head for problem-solving but he wanted to work, earn money and go travelling. We were good friends. Let's go and see the Skull this afternoon, to check out if the combination of your phone's light and music will have the same results as yesterday and if the girl will appear again. We'll take it from there. Call your mother, Matthew, and tell her that we're going to have lunch at McDonalds."

During their quick lunch the three adventurers were so worked up about their secret plan that they could hardly swallow their food.

At the exhibition they found the same large crowd and saw a billboard stating that the exhibition would be open only for two more days.

We have to act soon, we haven't got much time, went through their minds. Mr Harvey's well-planned action unfolded without a hitch.

They had a long wait in the queue, as expected, but when he figured they were one minute away from arriving at the Skull, he signalled to Matthew to reset the alarm on his phone.

As they reached the Skull Hannah dropped one of her earrings. She bent down and made some space around herself to look for it, which distracted the attention of the people from Matthew. On cue, the alarm on his phone went off, producing the same light and sound as the day before. As soon as the blue light reached the Skull, the figure of a young girl appeared. She made a begging gesture toward Matthew and mouthed some words. Mr Harvey translated her Quecha words as "take me away!"

Hannah made a show of finding her earring then the excited little group left the exhibition and returned to the Harveys' place.

"What are we going to do next," wondered Matthew, chewing his lips. "We've got to help her," he added with conviction.

"We have to do two things," his teacher said. "First we have to get the Skull, then we have to get out of Chicago. I have an idea. Matthew, go home and tell your mother that the principal called and said that two students did not show up when the group set off for the camp at the Mammoth Cave National Park. There are two free, paid-up places. Ask your Mom to let you come with me and Hannah tomorrow to join the camping. It's a three hour drive to get there."

"What do we want to do at the Mammoth Cave Park?" asked Matthew.

"Absolutely nothing." Seeing Matthew's confused face, Mr Harvey added, "I hope to arrange with Tony Vukic to get us the Skull by tomorrow morning and take it with us. "

Matthew was so surprised by the wild scheme that for a moment he stopped breathing, but he knew he was not going to back down, he will follow Harvey's plan. He looked at Hannah who stared at her father with wide eyed admiration.

"Once we've got the Skull," continued Harvey, we'll fly from the Chicago International Airport to Lima in Peru. There is a direct flight Chicago-Lima. The rest of our mission is not clear yet. A lot will depend on our captive Princess. In any case, we'll have at least two weeks without any disturbance to act because people will know from your mother that we are at the camp."

"I wonder what my Mom will say to this. "

"She'll stop worrying when she learns that I'm taking Hannah there with you. Every other day you'll be able to send e-mails to your Mom describing how happy you are at the camp. This white lie will prevent her getting worried about you.

"Even if we would fail in helping the Princess, which I doubt very much - after all, we are acting on a supernatural signal, a heavenly intervention - our little excursion with the Skull will not be treated as a 'theft', but as part of a scientific research excursion, - I hope."

"Are you sure we can get away with this adventure, Mr Harvey? I'm all for going ahead but I know Mom will be terrible worried."

"Go home, Matthew, and wait for my call which will signal that I managed to acquire the Skull. At the same time you can let me know if your Mom has agreed to you going on the free camping trip."

At 9 p.m. Bert Harvey phoned the Bolgers' and told Matthew that everything went according to plan and he will pick him up at 8 o'clock.

Mrs Bolger insisted on thanking Mr Harvey on the phone herself for taking care of Matthew and for the free camping trip.

Matthew hardly slept that night. His mind feverishly worked on various imaginary plans for the next fortnight.

Next morning, the Harveys came for Matthew in a station wagon filled with camping gear. After leaving Mrs Bolger, they drove to the Field Museum, where within minutes Tony Vukic met them carrying a small hat-box covered by his raincoat. He had the Skull in the box. Mr Harvey thanked Vukic for his help and promised to contact him in Canada, the way they agreed, as soon as the 'noise settled down.' Vukic left and the Harveys' car left the scene too, to be parked at the Chicago International Airport.

While on the way to the airport, Mr Harvey told the youngsters about his agreement with Tony Vukic. "Tony has relatives and a girlfriend in Canada. He's been planning to leave Chicago for some time. Last night the other guard wanted to go to a wedding and asked Tony to sign in for him and take over his night-shift.

"Every night after closing-time they took the Skull off the pedestal and placed it on the shelf under the display box. It was kept there in a hat-box filled with plastic bubble-wrap. There was another similar box under the shelf as a back-up in case the first box got damaged. Just before the 8 a.m. changing of the guard, Tony switched the boxes and smuggled out the box with the Skull covered by his raincoat.

"They will not discover that something is missing before 10 a.m. when they open the museum and want to put the Skull back on display. In the great excitement Tony forgot to tell me the password to the lock on the box but luckily I remembered to ask for it," Harvey told them, smiling.

Why is Mr Harvey calling the girl a Princess, wondered Matthew time and again. He received his answer during the trip.

"The girl couldn't have escaped her fate without the help of Shamans, and they are not giving life-saving help to just anybody.

She had to be member of the royal family. We're going to find out all details in time," explained his teacher.

CHAPTER THREE

THE PLANE TOOK THEM TO Lima with a short stopover in Miami. In Lima they took a cheap hotel for two days before they travelled on toward their target, Cuzco. Bert Harvey reasoned that this way, if there would be anybody tracking them, they would lose their trail.

In Cuzco, Harvey told the taxi driver to take them to the Terra Andina Hotel. "Is that the one we stayed at the last time?" asked Hannah. That was how Matthew found out that the Harveys had already visited Peru before.

To Matthew's questions Hannah explained that eight years ago she had come to Peru with her parents.

There was an accident and Hannah's mother fell from the Inca Trail on their way up to Machu Pichu. She died and was buried in Cuzco.

In the afternoon Hannah chased up the llamas from the surrounding meadow. The strange, awkward animals apparently took a liking to Hannah and escorted her back to the hotel.

Next day they visited Mrs Harvey's grave in the picturesque Cuzco cemetery which was on a steep incline. The gravesite had been kept in order and was surrounded by fresh flowers.

The tourists had dinner in the hotel restaurant, cold cuts and llama yoghurt. Matthew remarked, "These poor animals are used for everything here. They use them to carry loads, they use their milk, flesh, skin and hair."

Returning to their rooms after dinner Matthew found a Spanish note on his pillow. The Harveys translated it:

"Move to the Machu Pichu Pueblo Hotel. I will meet you tomorrow at the Intihuatana stone in Machu Pichu at midnight."

"What is this Intihuatana stone?" asked Matthew.

"Intihuatana means Hitching Post of the Sun. It used to be an astronomical observatory for the Incas. At two equinoxes, at midday on 20th March and 22nd September, the sun stands directly above the pillar, creating no shadow at all. For a moment it seems to be tied to the rock," explained Bert, then added, "it is the highest point in Machu Pichu."

"Somebody was here," they suddenly realized. "Where is the Skull?" they shouted in unison. They jumped to Matthew's wardrobe where under his sportswear, the hat-box with the Skull inside was hidden. At Harvey's suggestion they did not place the Skull into the hotel safe. *It would be unusual to put a hat-box into the safe and it would draw attention to it,* he thought.

"What now?" asked Matthew.

"Well, you were contacted. They know why you are here and I suppose they are willing to do a deal," said Harvey.

"Yes, but who are they? And I don't know exactly what we wish to do. I merely wanted to bring the poor prisoner Princess home. You must have wanted to decode the secret of the Skull. Okay, I suppose we'll have to go to the mountain and talk to these people, who ever they are. But what then?" worried Matthew.

"I suppose, first of all, we'll have to speak to the Princess and find out her situation and her wishes," said Hannah who hadn't said a word until now. The two men agreed. They locked the door, closed the windows and the curtains tightly.

"We'll have to speak quietly," Matthew warned the others and went to fetch the box.

He placed the box on the table and they sat around. "Well, what are you waiting for, open the box," Mr Harvey told Matthew.

"The code is triple nine, isn't it," said Matthew and looked around as if he waited for approval or contradiction. When the other two just nodded their approval, Matthew pressed the number nine button on the lock three-times. With a quiet click the box opened and there was the Skull.

"Take it out, for goodness sake," Harvey urged Matthew and when nobody moved, he got up, carefully took out the Skull from the box and placed it in the middle of the table.

On the table, under the hanging lamp, the Skull seemed to vibrate. It became foggy but as it absorbed more and more light, it became translucent. The three people sitting quietly around the table, drew their chairs closer to face the Skull.

Without saying a word Harvey moved his head and winked at Matthew, who took out his mobile phone, and looked at Harvey, as if waiting for further instruction. Harvey just nodded and Matthew set the alarm.

The air in the semi-dark room was sultry and oppressive as they waited. Then suddenly it lit up as if they were on stage. Strong blue light flooded the room. It seemed the blue light originated from the Skull and not from the screen of the phone. The haunting melody of *El Condor Pasa* sounded and the slender figure of a girl appeared inside the Skull. She was beautiful. Her long dark hair covered her shoulders, and she wore a pearl tiara.

"It's magic," murmured Hannah and Matthew under their breath. There was quiet for a while and the girl looked at the three with a questioning eye. Finally Hannah broke the silence. She spoke in Quecha to the Princess.

"We made a long trip in the hope that we'd be able to help you, though we don't even know whether you want us to help, or whether we'll be able to help you get what you want?"

"Who are you? How did you get inside the Skull?" Harvey interrupted Hannah's line of thought, speaking in English.

"I am Princess Cuxi Carpai of the Huascar Royal Family. My father was Huascar, my mother was the Coya, the first wife of Huascar. When my grandfather, Huayna Capac, died in 1527 there were two claimants to the throne, Huascar and his half-brother, Atahualpa, the son of one of Huyna's ordinary wives. Atahualpa started a civil war and he cruelly destroyed every member of the Huascar family."

"Were you killed too?" Matthew blurted out. The pressure on him was too much to bear quietly.

"Yes and No," answered the Princess. She continued her story after Matthew was warned to keep quiet and let the Princess tell her tale.

"I was a twin. I had a twin brother. He was named Meita Capac. At the time of our birth The Inca, Huyna Capac, was still alive and according to custom we were both taken away from our family at the age of four. Meita was taken to the Yachayhuasis House of Knowledge, to be brought up as an official, or as a soldier, and I was taken to the Virgins of the Sun Monastery in Cuzco. I never had any further connection with Meita. We wouldn't have met again except for the tragic event that occurred after Atahualpa won the civil war and ordered the killing of every member of Huascar's family.

"By the time I was about thirteen, the killing spree ordered by Atahualpa had reached the Cuzco Convent. Nobody thought that Atahualpa's murderers would dare to attack the Virgins of the Sun.

There were about 150 women in the convent under the supervision of one Shaman.

"One day the soldiers came, a Panaca (Royal relative) was the Captain. He told the Shaman that all the women would be killed but first his men had a choice of which women they wanted to enjoy before they killed them. He also told the Shaman that there was a boy who had just reached thirteen. His trial of manhood would be to subdue the most beautiful young girl in the convent.

"The Shaman took me to the Captain as the offering for the manhood trial. All the soldiers sat around and they led in the boy. He was nude. I was ordered to disrobe too. When at the crowd's encouragement the boy approached me I thought the Earth would open up and swallow me. It was Meita, my twin brother. We both had identical birthmarks under our left breast. I collapsed and lost consciousness."

"What happened then? Do you know what happened to your brother?" asked Hannah.

"When I came to, I was in the Pecaru cave, an ancient refuge in Machu Pichu. The Shaman told me that he brought another girl to satisfy the soldiers, and flew with me to Pecaru. I never heard of my brother again.

CHAPTER FOUR

"IN PECARU THE SHAMAN TOLD me that I couldn't live in Atahualpa's empire anymore, since he had ordered the killing of every member of my family. The Shaman offered to transport me into the Fourth Dimension where I could meet other unfortunates who were all prisoners of Time. I would not be able to communicate with people in the third dimension or with those in the Fifth, Ethereal Dimension. My only chance for communication would be through a colour/melody code. I would be able to communicate only with those who could discover the code and contact me that way."

"What happened then? That was five hundred years ago?" asked Matthew.

"The Shaman threw me down the Endless Shaft leading from Pecaru to Infinite Time. I woke inside the Crystal Skull.

"I lost all sensation. I was buried inside the Skull in a mountain. Later there was an earthquake that brought up the Skull to the surface. You are my first ever visitors."

"What could we do to help? asked Harvey.

"For me the only way out is to enter the Fifth Dimension where I could meet with the rest of my relatives murdered on Atahualpa's order. The Shaman could take me through the Golden Gate into the Fifth Dimension."

"Why would the Shaman, who kept you a prisoner for hundreds of years, help you to escape his power?" asked Matthew.

"I think that he, or they, whoever they are, are trying to get the Crystal Skull back. After the earthquake it slipped out of their hands."

"Do you think the Shaman would bargain with us, offering your freedom for the Skull?"

"I think so but I could be wrong and giving him back the Skull may help them to cause terrible upheaval."

"What terrible upheaval?" asked Hannah, disregarding her father's warning gesture not to continue the subject.

"It is the March of 2012 now. The prophecy is that 'the world will end on the 21st December this year. The original 13 Crystal Skulls have to be together to have that power. We don't know how many of the other Skulls are in the hands of the Shamans but maybe this is the only one they are missing to have power over the world."

"You better rest now, Princess. Tomorrow we will travel to meet the Shaman and see if we could get your freedom without risking a catastrophe," said Mr Harvey. He signalled to Matthew to put his phone away and the room receded into semi-darkness.

"Rest, think and sleep now, children. Tomorrow morning we'll take the train from Cuzco to Agua Callientes and from there we'll take a bus up to Machu Pichu. We'll have to be rested and think clearly when we meet the Shaman."

The three of them retired to their rooms and within minutes there was total quiet. After a little time there was knocking on Hannah's door. The maid entered. She warned Hannah to keep quiet.

"You have to go quickly and quietly to the Market. Leave the hotel in secret. Don't talk to anybody. At the end of the Market an old woman is selling brooches and hairpins. She is wearing a Condor face-mask. She is a Shura, the only woman Shaman in the Mountain. She has connection with the Spirits and she can defend families.

"Go and take the Skull with you. Don't be afraid. You are protected here by the Shura." With this she left.

Hannah was left with a terrible problem. Should she leave without telling her father? Should she risk taking out the Skull, which was in her wardrobe only accidentally because she changed rooms with Matthew? What would my mother want me to do? She posed the question to herself and felt that her mother would want her to go. She covered the box containing the Skull with a shawl and left for the Market.

Hannah found the Shura, the old woman, wearing a bird's mask. She signalled that she had the Skull with her.

"We are going to see your mother," said the Shura. She packed her wares and took Hannah up toward the cemetery.

Nobody was around in the small cemetery when they reached Mrs Harvey's grave. The Shura told Hannah to place the Skull on top of the grave and she started to mumble and pray. After a while she stopped praying and with closed eyes touched the tombstone. She kept her hands on the stone and called out. "Come, your daughter needs your advice."

She turned to Hannah and pointed at the Skull. Hannah saw her mother appear in the Skull. For a while she thought that she was dreaming.

"Ask her," said the Shura, waking her from her reveries.

Hannah told her mother about all circumstances of them coming to Cuzco and their doubt about how to deal with the Shaman's expected demands. Only when she finished the story of the Skull and the Princess, did she ask: "Where are you, how are you, what are you doing?"

"I'm in the Fourth Dimension, I am the prisoner of Time like your Princess. One day, when I might be able to move into the Fifth Dimension, I will learn everything about you, how you are and what you are doing. You don't have to worry about me, the Shura takes good care of me. About the Skull and the Shaman.: do not let the Skull fall into the Shaman's hands under any circumstances. He and his cohorts could destroy your world if they have all the 13 Skulls.

"Now I have to go. Don't try to visit me again and don't tell your father about our meeting. You are an adult and the Shura will advise you what to do in Machu Pichu with the Shaman and the Skull." With this she disappeared.

Hannah walked back to the hotel fast without meeting anybody. She lay down and fell asleep.

CHAPTER FIVE

In the morning Hannah's father knocked on her door.

"Get up, we don't have much time to catch the first train from Cuzco to Agua Callientes."

They had a quick breakfast and left the hotel. Hannah was carrying the box with the Skull. From Agua Callientes terminal a bus took them to Machu Pichu. It was another half an hour walk to the Machu Pichu Pueblo Hotel.

They spent the day walking around visiting the famous local relics, the Funerary Rock Hut, the Sun-Dial and the Temple of The Seven Rays. They walked up to the Hitching Post of the Sun, where they were expected to meet the Shaman at midnight.

The large carved rock emerged from a round base and was surrounded by a wire fence to keep the tourists away.

"What harm could tourists do to the massive stone?" Hannah asked her father.

"According to legend, people who touch their nose to the stone can hear voices or get an electric shock."

"Do you believe that Dad?"

"Yes, I think I do. Why take the risk?"

Before her father finished his warning, Hannah jumped over the wire and pressed her nose to the stone. Matthew and Harvey stiffened. They lost their voice watching Hannah's unexpected action. Within one minute Hannah returned and she was ready to explain her deed.

"We hear so many stories, quoting legends and we just walk by without testing any of them. This to me is like walking blindfolded without taking at least an occasional look at the marvels we pass by."

"Did you learn something by touching the stone?" asked Matthew.

"Yes, I did. I was told that the Shura will be here tonight and I should listen to her."

"Who is the Shura? Have you met her?" asked Matthew and Harvey together. They felt what may lay ahead of them was not getting any clearer, rather more obscure.

"She is the female Shaman who defends families. She knows why we are here and she has already warned me not to let the Crystal Skull slip into the Shaman's hand because it could be the last, the 13th Crystal Skull they need to rule and destroy our world."

After the day-long walks and climbing, the three adventurers were exhausted when at midnight they returned to the Hitching Post to meet the Shaman. They were disappointed. The Shaman came and immediately left after telling them to go to the Pecaru Caves where he'd be waiting. They had no choice but to walk another half an hour, luckily this time downhill. Hannah didn't see the Shura but heard her voice telling her, "The bottomless shaft is in the Pecaru Caves. Be very careful."

As soon as the three entered Pecaru Caves the Shaman appeared. He was a native South American with long black braided hair reaching past his shoulders. A shiny Sun-disc hanging from a gold chain around his neck covered his breast.

"Let me see the Skull," was the Shaman's first word.

"Don't let it out of your hands," the Shura warned Hannah. She was hiding in the shadows. Hannah uncovered the box and looked at her father for his approval to open it and let the Shaman see the Skull. When he nodded she opened the box and turned it toward the Shaman.

"Give it to me. I want to check it out. What are you afraid of?" The Shaman extended his arms to take the box.

"No!" her father cried out and pushed Hannah back, out of the Shaman's reach.

"First you have to guarantee that the Princess will be released from the Skull and can join her relatives in the Fifth Dimension. We'll light up the Skull to see that she really is released." With this Harvey signalled Matthew to set the alarm on his phone, but he was already on the job. Very soon the Princess appeared in the Skull.

"Order her release, and let her through the Golden Gate to join the Fifth Dimension."

"Alright, I order her release and permit her to pass through the Golden Gate."

As soon as the Shaman finished his words, the Princess waved goodbye to her rescuers and disappeared from the Skull.

The three could hardly believe that their long tiring mission had ended and felt like embracing each other. However, other dramatic events overtook their elation.

The Shaman stepped forward and bent down to grab the box with the Skull. He almost had it in his hands when with a lightning swoosh the Shura jumped from the shadows, grabbed the box and hurled the Shaman down head long into the bottomless well in the middle of the cave.

CHAPTER SIX

AFTER THE SHURA PUSHED THE Shaman into the bottomless well, the others looked to her for an explanation, or advice, but she had disappeared. "Let's go back to the hotel," said Harvey and, carrying the Skull very carefully, they left the Pecaru cave and set out for the half an hour trek to the Machu Pichu Pueblo Hotel.

"What now Dad?" asked Hannah.

"First of all we should have a good sleep after the day's excitement. I'll keep the Skull in my room. Tomorrow morning we'll have a talk about our next step," he said and left the exhausted youngsters.

Next morning they had a short breakfast. People sitting at the tables close by had prevented them from discussing their plans. After breakfast, Hannah and Matthew went into her father's room and sat at the table, gazing at the Skull box sitting there and waiting for him to open the discussion.

He sat between them and without hesitation moved the box into the middle of the table and opened the lock.

"We don't know if the Shaman, or somebody else, is making the decisions, or the Skull itself," blurted out Matthew impatiently and looked to his teacher for his opinion.

"You are right, Matthew. I guess it was unfair to drag you two into this affair without explaining the full implications. I suppose we cannot act with any degree of success without knowing and considering the full array of questions involved.

"The Skull is only an instrument of those who manipulate life on Earth in all its forms. There are other 'beings' involved who use the Shamans, and use the Skulls to their ends. Does this sound frightening? Does it sound strange, out of this world? It sure does because it is out of our world.

"You heard from me only about the interesting parts but not about the frightening parts. There is more to it!

"It is possible, my dear Hannah, that your beloved mother's death was not an accident. It may have been an act of revenge by the Shamans for my intrusion into their realm. Forcing the freedom of the Princess again interfered with their plans.

"It is my duty now to explain to you to the best of my knowledge what dangers you are exposing yourself to if you continue with me on this dangerous journey."

"Before we go any further," cut in Hannah, "I met with the Shura at her initiative here in Cuzco the other night and she called up my mother with the help of the skull.

"Mother told me that she was also in the fourth dimension like the Princess and warned me not to let the skull slip into the hands of the Shamans. Mom also told me not to tell anybody about our meeting," added Hannah when she saw that her father wanted to ask her something.

"I could tell you many other things about esoteric sciences and spiritualism and I promise you that I will, but first we have to decide whether we should probe deeper into the role of the Shamans and their use of the Crystal Skulls or whether we should concentrate on cleaning up traces of our role in acquiring the skull unlawfully and using it for our purposes."

"What do you suggest Mr Harvey ?" asked Matthew. Hannah quietly waited for her father's response.

"I suggest we should stop this research. You are both sixteen, your path should lead through matriculation and college before you decide what to do with your lives. If later you should decide to study esoteric sciences in depth, you'll still have plenty of time to do so. The subject goes back to thousands of years ago. There is no hurry to take it up. Well, do you agree?"

The youngsters agreed and there began a discussion of the details of their return.

The Lima-Chicago flight was uneventful. They picked up Harveys' car at the Chicago International Airport car park and drove to the Mammoth Cave National Park camping ground to cover up their absence.

CHAPTER SEVEN

THE FIRST STAGE OF THEIR planned return didn't go smoothly. "Where have you been, Bert?" asked Jim Barraclough, the camp director. "Matthew's mother sent three e-mails and phoned twice," he added.

"Matthew will phone his mother straight away and I'll tell you all about our little research excursion," said Bert and pulled his colleague aside.

Matthew's phone call was not successful. Instead of hearing his mother's voice, he heard a strange, accented voice say; "Think before you jump. Call again."

Who in the hell could that be? And what did he mean by, 'think before you jump?' I'll call my dad, was Matthew's first idea but as he saw Mr Harvey coming he decided to ask for his advice first.

"Wait, we'll have a discussion tonight and we'll decide then." They had an early dinner with the campers and withdrew to their sleeping quarters, claiming fatigue after the long trip.

They closed the curtains and locked the door in Mr Harvey's cabin. He placed the box with the Skull on the table and opened it. He took out the Skull and warned the youngsters to keep quiet. Pulling his chair close to the table, he placed his left hand on the top of the Skull. After a while a dull light lit up the eye sockets. Hannah and Matthew couldn't tear their eyes away from the Skull, which had started to look alive. Harvey's voice sounded eerie when he asked: "What happened to the boy's mother? Where is she?"

Hannah and Matthew didn't know what to expect. Would the Skull answer? Would it speak? They first stared at Harvey then at the Skull, but nothing happened. After a few minutes he put the Skull back into the box.

"What happened, Dad?" asked Hannah. He gave a little smile.

"Did you think you would hear the Skull speak?" The youngsters nodded. "It doesn't work that way. I received a telepathic message. Matthew's mother is in the hands of the Shamans and they offer to exchange her for the Crystal Skull. They didn't say where and how. We have to contact them tomorrow at the same time.

"My impression is that she was taken out of the USA.

"We have now 24 hours to prepare a good cover story for the next two weeks, where we're going and what we are going to do during the rest of the school holiday period."

The day passed slowly. Hannah and Matthew played volley ball with the campers and Bert discussed problems of camping with Jim. After an early dinner the three locked themselves in Hannah's Dad's cabin again. He put the Skull on the table, placed his left hand on the top of the Skull and asked for further details about the disappearance of Sarah Bolger. In the next few minutes Matthew and Hannah were watching her Dad who seemed to be listening intensely to a voice they couldn't hear. He finally nodded and took his hand off the Skull.

"Well, where is my mother? Where can we find her?" asked Matthew excitedly.

"She is all right now and the captors, obviously Shamans, want to exchange her for the Skull. It won't be easy, even if we agree, which we'll obviously have to," he said with a deep sigh.

"Common Dad, where is she? How can we find her?" asked Hannah impatiently.

"Well, it's like this," he said, then stopped for a moment before going on. "Matthew's mother has been kidnapped and taken to a faraway hiding place."

"How far? Outside the United States?" asked Matthew.

"Way outside the States. To Tibet."

"Tibet? Who did this? How did they get there? Are you sure they said Tibet?"

"Of course I am sure. They gave a more definite address too. They're keeping her in the Dharma Cave in the Red Hill in Lhasa. If we take the Skull there we'll be contacted."

"Do you think we could find that place, Dad?"

"It's not impossible, only very complicated."

"What are the problems Mr Harvey?" asked Matthew.

"Let me tell you the ones that come to mind. First, we need American passports and Chinese visas to enter Tibet. It is now Chinese territory, you know. You may remember the worldwide demonstrations against the brutal repression the Chinese exerted in Tibet during the 2008 Beijing Olympic Games."

"But Matthew can't get an American passport, he is under age," suggested Hannah.

"You are right. I could add you to my passport, you are under age too but Matthew could not get a passport without parental agreement. The solution? We have to slip through into Canada. Canadians do not need a visa to get into India, or Nepal."

"Why go to India?" asked Hannah and Matthew at the same time.

"We could never get a Chinese visa to get into Tibet. But there are about a hundred thousand refugees from Tibet in the North of India and Nepal, close to the Tibetan border, who left Tibet illegally and keep contact with their relatives, political and religious brethren. The Dalai Lama lives there too in Dharamsala."

"You talk about the general idea of how to get into Tibet, Dad, but what about money and contacts in Canada, in India and in Lhasa? I'm sure you have some ideas about those details too. Why don't you tell us about them now?"

"You are right, darling. I'll tell you a few details that will make you feel safer about this dangerous journey. First about Canada. You may not know, but I graduated first at the Waterloo University in Ontario, before I went to Yale. At Waterloo I studied in the Esoteric and Exoteric Sciences Faculty, where we experimented with Soul Transfer, Yoga, Buddhism and Spiritualism. We had teachers and students from India, Nepal and Tibet and I made some very good friends. Some were and I'm sure still are, Tibetan nationalists. I intend to get an official letter from the Waterloo University that I am on a research trip with my two assistants. My former student friends living now in India and Nepal will assist us to cross the Nepal-India border and give us further contacts for our journey into Tibet.

"This much should be enough for you for tonight. Let's get a good sleep. Tomorrow we'll have to leave early; I'll have to take out money from the bank."

Chapter Eight

At breakfast the atmosphere was good. They knew now what they had to do, though they still didn't know how they'd be able to do it. Bert Harvey seemed confident and the youngsters had complete trust in him.

"The only thing I heard about Buddhism was the saying; Om Mani Padme Hum. I don't think that will get me far," said Hannah and looked at her father waiting for his reaction.

"*Behold the jewel in the lotus!* That is the translation of that mantra in the interpretation of the Dalai Lama.

"Originally it is in Sanskrit. There are many other translations too. The believers are supposed to repeat it as many times a day as they can, turning their prayer-wheels as they say it. It is supposed to turn your imperfect body and mind into the same perfection as the Buddha's."

After breakfast Bert phoned Waterloo University in Ontario. A wide smile on his face told the watching Matthew and Hannah that her father's old friend, Evan Godfrey, was still at Waterloo. "We are welcome in Ontario, children," he told them.

After a long drive, crossing into Canada in their car, they arrived at Waterloo where Bert Harvey's old school-mate waited for them and took them to the rooms he arranged at the University campus.

They had a light supper at the university cafeteria and Bert went with Evan Godfrey into his office to discuss further plans. On his advice, Hannah and Matthew retired to their rooms. Leafing through the brochures they found in the room, they learned that Waterloo was founded by German migrants and had a population of about 90,000, including the university students. They studied the photos of the wide clean streets, realizing that they'd have no time for sight-seeing the following morning.

Mr Harvey told them at breakfast that they were on their way! He'd already made bookings with Air Canada which had direct flights from Ontario airport to Kathmandu in Nepal, close to the Tibetan border, where a couple of his former Tibetan school-mates lived and worked for the Tibetan refugees.

"We've got the papers too," he added and took out a letter on a Waterloo University letterhead which read:

This is to certify that Professor Bert Harvey of the Waterloo University is conducting archaeological research in the Nepal-Tibet area with two junior assistants employed on a temporary basis by the University. Help provided to the team would be greatly appreciated. Benjamin Ottamar, Vice-Chancellor.

After saying goodbye to Mr Godfrey the team drove to the Ontario airport where they sold the old car to the local car dealer. "We won't be coming back this way," he explained.

The flight to Kathmandu with a short refuelling stop in Bangkok took ten hours. It was strange for the travellers that on account of the ten hour time – zone difference travelling westward from Ontario -

they arrived at Kathmandu in the Tribhuvan International Airport at the same hour as they left. They were sleepy and felt jet-lagged.

Harvey told the driver of a knocked-about three-wheeled Tuk-Tuk that they wanted to go to the Kathmandu Guest House and in fifteen minutes, shaken by the badly paved roads, they arrived at the Guest House given to Bert as their first point of contact. The trip cost them 75 Nepalese Rupees, 1.50 US dollars. Mr Kishor Shrestna, the manager, was an old friend from the Waterloo University.

The travellers had a well deserved rest during what was left of the day and met Mr Shrestna for dinner, at his invitation.

After recalling mutual memories from their university days Bert told his old friend the cover story he'd made up. "The University received a letter from Lhasa about the discovery of a valuable historic document. To prevent it getting into the hands of the Chinese occupiers it was arranged for it to be passed it on to a delegate of the University, someone who would personally ask for it."

"I understand the significance of your mission and we Tibetan refugees will give you all the help we can. You have to be aware that your mission is quite dangerous. I will have to ask the help of other Tibetans, the organizers of our underground missions, to get you over the border in secret and get you to Lhasa. I will do this tomorrow. You can have a rest before you set out on your long, tiring journey. Why don't you try our national dish 'Pad Thai' while you are here?"

The travellers enjoyed the spicy rice dish prepared with Tamarind and Sweet Chilli in fish sauce.

The garden restaurant was spotless and the table settings rivalled the best restaurants they'd seen in the States. The surrounding palm trees completed the tropical atmosphere.

The next day Hannah and Matthew did some leisurely sightseeing. They walked along the narrow streets with colourful stalls selling everything from silk shawls to fancy copper and silver wares. They admired the huge flat round Buddhist temple with its strange, irregular shaped central tower. They were surprised to see that some of the traffic and the selling was done on canals, which they didn't know existed in Kathmandu. They had well deserved rest after the long tiring walk in the heat of the day and met with Hannah's Dad only in the evening at the restaurant.

He came early to meet them and told them about things he had discovered during the day. "Everything is cheap if the price is converted into US Dollars. There are three ways to travel from Kathmandu to Lhasa: air, rail and buses. Of course everything will depend on Mr Shrestna," he reported.

Mr Shrestna arrived and without ordering his meal he started to explain what he considered important for the tourists to know.

"Your travelling will have to be done by bus because it is the slowest and we are best organized to carry out missions using the bus route. You may wonder why the slowest route is the best. Acclimatization! Lhasa is over 3600 metres high. The air is much rarer, there is much less oxygen. A sudden change could be fatal for some people. Railways and buses have to carry oxygen cylinders to care for emergency cases. You have to know which bus companies guarantee to take oxygen with them to be safe.

"You must carry at least 100 US Dollars or the equivalent Chinese Yuan with you. One Dollar is eight Yuan. In Tibet some merchants will accept only Yuan and more importantly you must have Yuan in case you'll have to bribe Chinese soldiers.

"The trip will take five days. Our guide will escort you to the end. He knows the routes, the bus crews and most importantly, he knows the Chinese soldiers who will check the bus at the usual stations.

"Other problems are to prepare warm clothing and food. You'll be able to buy some food from the bus staff but for safety's sake you should take tinned food with you.

"You men shouldn't shave and you, dear," he pointed to Hannah, "shouldn't use any makeup or elaborate hairdo. The less conspicuous you look, the better for your safety. You may think that I am exaggerating but I saw many cases when people paid with their lives for being negligent.

"The Chinese Embassy will issue visas only for groups not for individuals. Single people would have to join others to make up at least a group of five. We'll organise the group and we'll get the visas for you.

"I have to warn you that the journey from Kathmandu to Lhasa is always an adventure. The road is poorly constructed. It is prone to closures by landslides. It can be very dusty and some kind of face mask is a good idea. As you drive up to 17,000 feet at some points, altitude sickness is a real possibility. Most people feel some of the symptoms. You must drink plenty of non-alcoholic liquid to help you acclimatize. Each night you will have to stop and stay at simple roadside hotels.

"There are strict controls over taking pictures inside the monasteries but upon paying a fee, a monk may allow it. Do not carry pictures of the Dalai Lama, Tibetan posters, Tee shirts, political magazines, or books.

"Well, that's about it. You will leave by bus the day after tomorrow at 5.30 am. I will introduce you to your guide tomorrow morning. He is a very experienced man.

CHAPTER NINE

IN THE MORNING MR SHRESTNA returned to the hotel with two men. The older one looked about fifty and the younger about twenty-five years old. "They will be your guides. Father and son, but they will travel under different names. The young guy is going to set up an anti-Chinese organisation in Lhasa but will tell the Chinese that he is going to visit his relatives. With the three of you they will make up a group of five, the smallest permitted tourist group. They both speak English and Chinese. They will be able to help you whatever problem should come your way."

"How many people will there be altogether in the group?" asked Harvey.

"The bus will take twenty passengers. A group of fifteen German tourists will join you, young boys and girls. Some speak English. You don't have to communicate much with them. If they ask awkward questions, pretend you don't understand."

The day passed quickly going around the markets and shops, buying tinned food, biscuits, one-litre canteens for each of them, warm woollen shawls. Hannah even bought a woollen pullover with wildflowers embroidered on it.

They got up at five the next morning to get to the assembly point, the Central Bus Terminal, by 5.30.

Chung Tsering, the father, and his son, Tensing, took them to the bus where the German group had already taken the best seats, leaving them the last row where according to common wisdom the shaking of the seats overhanging the rear wheels was the worst.

The bus started out on the Highway No.3. They call it Peace Highway, the guide informed them. In the Kathmandu Valley the road ran parallel with the Kyichu River. The first stop was at Kadari, the Nepal-Tibet border. From there they drove up to Zhangmu, the Chinese Immigration Post. This consisted of two wooden huts attended by half a dozen Chinese soldiers.

For unexplained reasons, the bus stopped about two kilometres short of the checkpoint and the passengers were warned to take all their luggage for inspection, because the bus would be searched after they disembarked and all prohibited items would be confiscated.

Matthew and Hannah smiled gratefully at her father when they realized he had foreseen this problem. He had bought them three identical backpacks at the Kathmandu market and told them to make an indelible capital B mark on a piece of material, and make a small flap of it which could be displayed or tucked inside the backpack. They kept the Skull in one of the backpacks which they kept back when the other two were taken up for inspection one by one, mixing with the other tourists. They returned for inspection again with one of the backpacks marked with the B, which the Chinese soldiers had already seen.

The passengers spent the night at the Zhangmu Hotel, a small wooden hut with ten small rooms. The tourists were set up two-by-two of the same sex in each room. Mr Harvey and Matthew kept the Skull with them, and never let it out of their sight.

The service consisted of hot water given to the tourists to make their own tea and a rough army blanket for the crude iron beds.

On the second day, the bus drove uphill till they reached Xegar. First they crossed Nyalamu Pass, then Lalung-La Pass. The Chinese driver said something to the German tourist sitting next to him which was translated by the guide as "this place is called the roof of the world." Looking at the breathtaking panorama of the Himalayan mountain ranges crowning the plateau they understood why it was called that. The Xegar Hotel was a perfect imitation of the Zhangmu Hotel/Guardhouse, including the 'service.'

The third day they drove from Xegar to Xiagtse. During the scenic drive they reached and crossed the Gyatchu-La Pass. The Pass is at 5220 metres, the highest on the way to Lhasa, they learned, by courtesy of the driver. At night they enjoyed the comfort of the Xigatse Hotel, another 'twin' of the two 'hotels' the tourists had already experienced.

On the fourth day, from Xiagtse to Gyantse, the tourists had their first pleasant surprise.

Soon after they set off in the morning they drove into the Panchen Lama's Tashi Lumpu Monastery.

In the austere building at least two-hundred saffron-clad monks were praying, kneeling with eyes closed. The monks' monotonous humming reminded Matthew of the sound of bees in a hive. Before dusk they reached the Phadkor Monastery which presented a similar picture and the passengers started to become nervous worrying that they would not reach their next night stop before dark. At night they enjoyed the same comfort in the roadside hotel as they had the previous nights.

The last day, on the road from Gyantse to Lhasa, the whole day was filled with watching the breathtaking panorama, the surrounding 4,500 to 5,000 metre high peaks. The colourful Yamdrok Lake, the Kyichu and the Brahmaputra Rivers looked almost unreal as the rays of the sun broke through the veil of the fog rising from the waters. To the disappointment of all passengers they had to spend the last night of the tour in another guardhouse/hotel. They were allowed to enter Lhasa only in the morning.

The thin air felt harsh and the sun's rays were intense. "They call Lhasa Sunlight City and the radiation is extremely strong," the guide told the group, who were searching for their sunglasses. Before entering the outskirts of the city they had to cross the Lhasa River, called by the locals the merry blue waves, the guide said.

The travel weary passengers were happy to learn that all of them had bookings at the same hotel, the Tibet Shannan Hubei Hotel on the Mid Beijing Road in central Lhasa. On their way to the hotel the guide explained the city of Lhasa was surrounded by three concentric circle paths. The innermost is called Nangkor, it contains the Jokhang Temple and the most sacred statue of Tibetan Buddhism. The middle circle is Barkor, passing through the Old Town. The outer Lingkor, encircles the entire traditional city of Lhasa.

The Shannan Hubei Hotel was a huge, modern building that looked anachronistic in the old town. Well-trained porters led the tourists through the reception area and showed them to their rooms. Mr Harvey and Matthew occupied a double room and Hannah had an adjacent single room.

They looked around the rooms and were satisfied that they had all the comfort tourists were used to in international hotels. Air conditioning, television, telephone, Internet access, mini-bar, bathroom. They soon checked and found everything in working order.

"What's the next step, Dad?" asked Hannah.

"Our contact here is the Manager, Mr Lobsang Gyatsen. Of course we don't know him. He has to contact us."

He had hardly finished the sentence when the doorbell rang. A man of medium height, in his early 40s, introduced himself:

"Lobsang Gyatsen. I received the message and I'm ready to help you. Tell me, what can I do for you?"

Harvey told him the same cover story they had used in Nepal:

an important ancient manuscript has been found by members of the resistance and they are willing to give it to him so he can take it to the HQ of Tibetan resistance.

"How is the meeting organised? How will you recognise the man? It could be a provocation. Where will you meet, do you have a password?"

The youngsters, unaccustomed to secret meetings, passwords and such, just looked at Harvey, with their mouths open. He, on the other hand, realized that Mr Lobsang's questions were relevant in such situations and put his mind to rest by saying that everything was organised. "We have to go to the Saint's Chapel in the Dharma cave, they'll contact us there with the password and will lead us to the place where they hide the document."

"This seems to be alright but first some steps have to be taken to allay any suspicion that may arise. The Chinese are watching closely every Westerner. One has to buy a ticket at least three days beforehand for a particular day. I will get the tickets for you.

"The three of you should go everywhere together. A family group looks less suspicious.

"I will have to warn you about local customs eagerly watched by the guards," continued Mr Lobsang.

"You have to tour the grounds clockwise, don't step on the door-sill, don't smoke in the halls, don't take photos without permission. Only 2,300 tourists a day are allowed to enter the Potala Palace. One group every 20 minutes. Go slowly. It is not easy for visitors to climb to the top building because of its height. The halls are always chilly. You had better take greatcoats.

"The Saints Chapel in the Dharma Cave is in the middle of the Red Palace. The Saints Chapel is on the third floor. There they worship Chenrezi, the bodhisattva of compassion. You will have to know all the details only when you have your tickets to the Palace. Use the next two days for sightseeing. If you need me for something, just ask for the Manager. I will bring your tickets to the Palace in time.

"One more thing, whether it will mean anything to you, I don't know. We suspect that one of the guards is a Shaman. Don't ask which one, we don't know. That's all. I will see you when I've the tickets for you.

CHAPTER TEN

USING THE TOUR GUIDE BROCHURE left in all rooms, the three Americans spent their time by first visiting the Grand Square in front of the Palace, then the Drepung Monastery, one of the greatest monasteries in Tibet. The monastery was established in 1416 by Yamjang Qoigyi who became the first Kampo (Director) there, teaching both Esoteric and Exoteric Buddhism.

"What is the difference between Esoteric and Exoteric Buddhism, Mr Harvey ?" asked Matthew.

"Esoteric means inner consciousness that is, considered from a mystical or meditative or contemplative perspective (eso-inner), while Exoteric (exo-outer) is the opposite and means everyday consciousness, that is, from a conventional perspective.

"Oh," said Matthew and looked at Hannah to see if she understood what her father was talking about.

In the grounds of the Monastery they are investigating the temples which Yamjang Qoigyi built in caves, including two magnificent white pagodas.

All members of the little group were exhausted by the time they returned to their hotel. They were happy to take off their backpacks. Mr Harvey insisted on them wearing the backpacks outside the hotel, to entice any Chinese who might follow them, into false security. They would think they always wore their backpacks and thus allay any suspicion they might have about them wearing backpacks in the Palace. No one would suspect one of the backpacks had the Skull in it.

Hannah complained that they had missed out on visiting the market, where she hoped to buy some Tibetan souvenirs.

Her father noticed that Matthew had drown back into a corner, staring into the distance with a gloomy face.

"Is something bothering you, Matthew? If it is your mother's situation, you should be satisfied that we're doing everything to save her. You've been downcast all day. What's on your mind? Tell us, maybe we'll be able to clear up your worry."

"It's just that all the time we are talking about saving my Mom. And that's of course my main worry. But how are we planning to free her? By giving the Shamans the Crystal Skull? The Shura in Machu Pichu and Hannah's mother in Cuzco warned us not to give the Skull to the Shamans because they could destroy the world if they obtain the Crystal Skull. This would mean that we not only didn't secure the survival of my mother, we actually helped the Shamans to destroy others, maybe the whole world! How could we allow this to happen?"

Hannah looked at her father waiting for his words to calm Matthew.

"I understand your worry, Matthew, but some facts should ease your soul. There are many, often conflicting theses and experiences that prevent us being sure which one presents the real truth.

"The theory of the Crystal Skulls is known from the Mayan and Inca legends. Even if we accept that the Mitchell-Hedges Skull is the 'kingpin' necessary in addition to the other twelve skulls, to give total power to the Shamans, we shouldn't forget that so far only eight of the twelve Crystal Skulls have been discovered and they are in the hands of various individuals who insist on keeping them.

"Now, back to our responsibility in letting the Crystal Skull fall into the hands of the Shamans. Be satisfied that I have a few tricks in mind to get your Mom released without strengthening the hands of the Shamans.

"This discussion has been a lesson for me not to tell you important things only in part, risking that you may draw the wrong conclusions.

"By the way, the 21st December 2012 date for the 'end of the world' is merely a speculative date taken from the Maya Long Calendar.

"At their peak, the Maya civilisation covered the northern parts of Central America (AD250-900). They were marvellous astronomers. They set up the Long Count Calendar in about 355BC arbitrarily, and it began with 0.0.0.0.0., which corresponded to August 11, 3114 BC. 1.0.0.0.0. was about 400 years. A date of 13.0.0.0.0. covered about 5126 years from the starting point and that would take us to December 21, 2012. All sorts of claims were made for this date. They range from 'nuclear holocaust' to Harmonic Convergence of Cosmic Energy flowing through the Earth, cleansing it and raising it to a higher level of vibration.

"Keep in mind that when a calendar comes to the end of a cycle it just rolls over into the next cycle. December 21st is not followed by the 'end of the world' but by December 22nd. So, 13.0.0.0.0. in the Mayan Calendar would be followed by 13.0.0.0.1 or December 22, 2012.

"According to another Mayan prophecy, Man is destined to bring about the end of the world on 21st December 2012. To counteract this, the Mayans carved 13 Crystal Skulls and sent them around the world; when they are reunited the world can be saved from oblivion.

"But that's enough for now. Let's eat something and have a rest. I have more useful programmes for tomorrow."

The small group had breakfast at nine o'clock. Thick fog covered Lhasa so they could not see the town from the hotel terrace.

"Let's go up into my room and clear up a few questions," said Mr Harvey.

CHAPTER ELEVEN

"WHO ARE THE SHAMANS?" ASKED Bert Harvey and when nobody answered him, he answered himself.

"Every time our path has been crossed by Shamans we learn about some crime they've committed. Kidnapped the Princess 500 years ago, kidnapped Matthew's mother recently, using her to blackmail us into returning the Crystal Skull to them, to be used for unimaginable crimes against humanity. Who are they? Are they the Masters, or only Servants in the big game of life? Who is directing them and for what purpose?

"Theoretically speaking Shamanism refers to a range of beliefs and practices concerned with communication with the spirit world.

"They are acting in the belief that spirits can play important roles in human lives. Spirits can be good or bad.

"Shamans engage in various techniques to incite trance (singing, dancing, drumming, etc.). The Shaman claims that his spirit leaves his body and enters into the supernatural world.

"Shamans can be healers too, they can treat illnesses. This is supposed to be done by traversing the Axis Mundi and forming a special relationship with the spirits. Shamanistic traditions have existed throughout the world since prehistoric times.

"Shamanism is based on the premise that the visible world is pervaded by invisible forces or spirits that affect the lives of the living."

"What is the Axis Mundi, Mr Harvey? I don't know about Hannah, but I never heard about it," said Matthew.

"According to the myths in many cultures, at the earliest stage the human life was one of the total harmony and wisdom. The planet was connected to the sky, which was always a place of light and the focus of human devotion.

"The trees and the mountains were the bridges, the connections, the Axis Mundi, the axle of the world.

"Humans could effortlessly communicate with the gods above. They could pass between heaven and Earth without obstacle because there was no death yet. The easy communication was cut off by a 'fall' from grace similar to that in the Christian bible. Since this 'fall', the only way to cross that bridge is in 'spirit'. In ecstasy, or when dead.

"By the way, Tibetan Buddhist monks have some special ways known only to them. You have probably never heard of 'soul transfer'. We dabbled in it at the Waterloo University in Canada. Jason Pang was our tutor. We managed it up to a point. It was probably more autohypnosis than soul transfer but the Tibetans could achieve it. First I read about it in Sven Hedin's book; *Travelling in the mysterious Tibet*.

"All I recall is that two monks were sitting in a dark cell in yoga position, staring into each others eyes. After one week their souls occupied the other's body.

"Mr Lobsang Gyatsen warned us about one Shaman parading as a monk here, but there could be other Shamans in Lhasa we should worry about, who are appearing to be monks."

In the ensuing quiet Harvey realized that he hadn't given a satisfactory explanation to Matthew's and Hannah's questions. He took a deep breath and continued.

"You are asking whether the Shamans who crossed our path so far were acting for local interests or were acting on 'superior orders'. You don't realize what is involved in searching for an answer to your question. Historians, astrologers, astrophysicists, archaeologists, geologists, cryptologists and other specialized scientists are all searching for that answer, and have been for centuries.

"The questions they have to find the answers to are: when and how was the Universe born, the birth and development of the celestial bodies, in particular the Earth, our Solar system, our closest and distant neighbours.

"There is no argument that there is a continuous development of everything, birth, maturity and death but we are unable to establish chronologically the stages of how the celestial bodies developed from chaos, how the Earth developed into a globe, how the continents and the oceans developed, how the micro-cosmos, the first life-forms, the single cells developed into higher life forms.

"Perhaps it is strange that after thousands of years of research, our best clues still could be found in mythology, the oral history of the ancient native people who lived and still live on various continents, who transmitted from mouth to mouth the description of the global and the celestial events their ancestors observed and survived.

"Using various names and different symbolism the creation myths all start with , 'in the beginning there was chaos', described as swirling fog. The clouds of swirling gases became denser and denser, absorbed the free cosmic dust and finally settled into rotating globes. The 'Creator' then called into being the celestial bodies, including the Earth, and ordered there to be land, water, flora and fauna, and finally created the first man and woman.

"In the infinite space the celestial bodies did not have regular orbits and from time to time they collided. In the process they ruined or damaged the weaker ones and these collisions threw them out of their previous orbits. This explains why the ancient astronomers fixed the positions of the Constellations in relation to each other differently.

"As human knowledge was widening, particularly after the discovery of ancient monuments, pyramids and the Nazca Lines in Peru, (which could be observed only from great heights) and rock-paintings, presenting humanoid figures with 'equipment' unknown at the time, it was reasonable to regard these objects as 'remnants of visits by more developed beings', who visited the Earth.

"The constellation of Orion was formed roughly 1.5 million years ago. It was recognized as a coherent constellation by many ancient civilizations and invoked various mythologies. The Sumerians, ancient Chinese, Mexicans, Indians and Australian Aborigines gave the constellation various names. The Yolngu people of Arnhem Land called Orion 'Julpan'.

"The Orion constellation is one of the longest observable constellations parallel to the rise of human civilization.

"In most ancient myths Orion is presented as a Hunter. In Greek, Egyptian and other myths there are detailed descriptions about Orion, the Hunter's adventures and love affairs which led to clashes with the Gods and finally led to his placement in the sky as a star.

"Connecting the stars of the Orion constellation produces a stick figure with club and shield. The two rhomboids representing his upper and lower torso are joined by three stars in a diagonal line like a belt.

"In some myths they talk about people from Orion, calling them 'Ant People' on account of their slender waist. Scryers and psychometrists tell stories about interventions by Orion people in the Earth in the past.

"So, my answer to your question, whether the Shamans we had the bad luck to meet with are of this Earth or of the Orion, my answer is: We don't know.

"Let's keep our eyes and ears open and let's get out of the way of these beings as fast as we can."

CHAPTER TWELVE

FOLLOWING MR LOBSANG'S ADVICE, THE small group took a taxi to the upper entrance of the Palace and got there before nine o'clock, the official daily opening time. There was already a large group of tourists waiting. Hannah counted them to check whether there were more than sixty. She knew from Mr Lobsang that the tourists were allowed to enter in groups of sixty every twenty minutes. Judging by their loud conversations there were a lot of Germans and a few Americans in the group.

Though they were warned, they do not know who Lobsang's undercover man is all three looked around trying to guess who their secret escort is. In addition to the German and American groups, there were also uniformed Chinese soldiers and four Tibetans dressed in ragged Western tourist outfits.

"I've got our man," said Matthew and pointed at a Tibetan who looked maybe thirty years old and wore a colourful knitted cap with strings hanging down over his ears. "He is the only one who kept eye contact, the others all turned away."

"You could be right but I'm not so sure," Harvey said, and kept studying the other Tibetans.

Looking around, they were satisfied that the advice to wear their backpacks at all times was correct. All tourists wore backpacks.

At exactly nine o'clock, a uniformed Chinese man stepped forward. He had no sign of rank on his uniform. He announced first in German then in English that he would be the guide for the tour and warned the tourists to stay with the group, not to wander away, not to take photos and not to smoke. "If you have any questions, buy the brochure at the kiosk, don't bother me," he finished his bilingual speech.

Luckily for the tourists, the group proved large enough to make private conversations possible without drawing the guide's attention. One American man proved to be quite knowledgeable. "I bet he is a history teacher, besides he's got the official brochure in his hand," pointed out Harvey.

"In 614, when Tibetan King Songstan Gambo married Princess Wencheng of the Chinese Tang Dynasty and Princess Bhrikuti of Nepal, he had two temples built for his two wives. Through his marriages he converted to Buddhism. Only two buildings of the original palace remained: The Cave for the Prince of Dharma and the Main Hall," explained the American.

On hearing about the 'Cave', Matthew, Hannah and her Dad pulled their coats tighter around them and looked into each others eyes significantly. They felt that the end of their mission was approaching.

The first hall the tourists entered was the Western Audience Hall. The huge garishly decorated hall's ceiling was supported by eight tall, square pillars richly covered by paintings, carvings and gold reliefs. The walls were covered by paintings of famous lamas. Something drew Matthew's attention. A Tibetan man was staring at him. At first Matthew was surprised by the man's uncommon behaviour then by looking at the man he had the feeling that the man did not belong to the group. One, two, three, four, five, Matthew counted the Tibetans. *We only had four of them at the start! Something is fishy. I'd better tell Mr Harvey ,* he decided.

Next they descended into the Eastern Sunshine Chamber which enjoyed plenty of sunshine through its large windows. From the balcony they could see a view of the whole of Lhasa. Well-worn wooden steps connected the two large halls. Looking around, the tourists could see tombs containing the remains of eight Dalai Lamas, well decorated shrines and chapels. The bodies of the eight previous Lamas were kept in gold-plated stupas.

Badly eroded steps went down into the next floor that was already part of the Red Palace above which the White Palace was built. "Only two sections of the original buildings remained inhabitable during the past stormy history; the Cave for the Prince of Dharma and the Main Hall, the Pagbalhakang Hall," quoted the American tourist.

On third floor of the Red Palace, the earliest part of the Potala Palace, a room was built in a cave for the memory of the First Tibetan King Songstan Gambo and his wife Princess Wencheng. Their statues were still standing in the room where the King used to pray.

"Caves in the Tibetan mountains played a major role in history. Whole cave-systems were discovered lately, twenty or thirty cave systems containing paintings, pottery, Tibetan scripts in ink which go back to the 13th century, gold and silver pieces from the pre-Christian era," explained the knowledgeable American.

This could be the place where my mother is kept, thought Matthew. He looked at Mr Harvey who had the same idea. *What next?* wondered the three. As usual, Bert Harvey had an idea how to proceed.

"Excuse me, Mr Guide," he addressed the Chinese guide, "could we see some of the treasures kept in the caves? It is twelve o'clock, the morning session is already finished, you must be tired. I'm a history teacher, I'm sure there are other teachers in the group too. This is our only chance of a lifetime to learn more about Tibetan history and to teach western students what a wonderful job the Chinese government has done in preserving part of Asia's glorious past. I'm sure we would be willing to pay extra money to you or the other guide who will take over from you at three o'clock. How about it?

"Be generous and give us a hand to help the Western students to understand the wonderful history of China."

Then he looked around to check the effects of his words on the rest of the tourists. All Westerners were nodding in agreement and the American teacher winked at him, approving his bold approach.

CHAPTER THIRTEEN

THE FACE OF THE CHINESE guide clearly showed his emotions as he struggled to decide whether to accept the money, the bribe, or keep his hostile, distrusting attitude toward the tourists. Finally his greed won the battle.

"Those Westerners who are willing to pay an extra 20 RMB can stay here and wait for the afternoon guide," he said in English. "Chinese and Tibetans can stay or return with me without paying," he added in Chinese. With this he left, followed by all the Chinese and the Tibetans with the exception of the fifth Tibetan who was suspected of having a role in Mrs Bolger's kidnapping.

"Clever Chinese guy," said the American referring to the guide, "he shared the responsibility with his partner. We'd better stay in one group to be covered if the crafty Chinese want to claim that something went missing while we were alone. What do you say, Mister?" He turned to Bert Harvey who became the unelected head of the group after his successful maneuver with the guide.

"Bert Harvey, history teacher from Chicago," was the way he introduced himself.

"Fifty of us in this smallish room is too many even to lie down. I suggest we form small groups who can watch out for each other, and they could either lie down or look around, but they should not wander far away. After all, we don't know the place, and we don't know our hosts either. Better be careful."

After these words, the large group broke up and formed smaller groups with noisy German and English arguments. Matthew and Hannah stayed close to her Dad. They realized that this could be the moment when the Shaman could approach them to go ahead with the promised switch.

In a minute the 'fifth' Tibetan approached Bert Harvey and signalled to follow him. He disappeared behind the statue of the first Tibetan King. The three closely followed through the narrow opening in the rocks behind the statue.

They found themselves in a small cave that had a larger opening at the back. The man quickly moved through the cave and entered the larger cave through the second opening. There was complete silence and the darkness was only broken by the uncertain light of a torch in the second cave.

It took time for the trio to get their bearings in the darkness. A couple of metres outside the circle of the torch light, a human shape stood, tied to a stake. It is Mom, thought Matthew, before the prisoner lifted her head and all three of them recognised Sarah Bolger.

They moved involuntarily forward but stopped immediately. They didn't see in the dark that they were standing on the edge of a deep crack in the rock, about three metres wide and five to six metres long. There was no way forward.

The Shaman, standing on the other side of the crack stepped forward and called out to the small group. "There she is. You can have her if you give us the Skull. Do you have it on you? Show me."

"We have the Skull here," said Harvey and lifted up his backpack, as if he had the Skull in it. In fact, the Skull was in Matthew's look-alike backpack.

"How do you want to finalize the exchange?" he asked.

"I hold out a pole over the crack and you tie on to it the box with the Skull in it. As soon as I check out the Skull, I lay a wide plank over the crack and she can walk over to you."

"No deal. I don't trust you. First untie her and let her come to the crack so we can speak to her. Maybe it is not even the same woman."

"Show me the Skull first!"

"Alright," said Harvey and turned around showing that he is taking his backpack off. In fact, he quickly exchanged his backpack with Matthew's which had the Skull in it. He opened the backpack, and the box, and showed the Skull to the Shaman.

"Here, have a look! First, place the plank over the crack and let her step on it. As soon as she takes the first step on the plank I'll throw the backpack over to you with the Skull. You don't have to worry. I wouldn't risk her life for the Skull."

While the Shaman untied Mrs Bolger, took her to the crack and placed the plank over it, Harvey changed back the backpacks and when Mrs Bolger made her first step on the plank, Harvey threw the empty backpack well out of the Shaman's reach so he couldn't check the contents before Matthew's mother reached her son.

"Quick, back to the group," ordered Harvey and they started to run."

"You don't have to run," said a Tibetan man stepping out of the shadows. "I will hold him up. Lobsang told you that we will help you. We keep our word. Go and get out of the Palace as soon as you can."

CHAPTER FOURTEEN

WITHOUT LOOKING BACK, THEY RUSHED Mrs Bolger through the little cave connecting to the Kings Chapel, bypassed the waiting tourist group without telling them a word and moved fast toward the entrance of the Palace.

Mrs Bolger was covered in Hindu fashion, in a long white sari from head to toe. Harvey told her to cover her face as if she had a coughing fit when they passed through the gates between the Chinese guards.

She did as she was told and Mr Harvey signalled to the guards that she had an attack and had to be taken into the city. They took a taxi that had just deposited some tourists and in 25 minutes they were back in the hotel.

Lobsang came to their room as soon as they phoned him. For the quickest departure, he suggested they fly from the Lhasa Airport to Kathmandu. The next plane was leaving in two hours and Lobsang ordered the four tickets on the phone.

They all thanked Lobsang for all the help provided by him and his comrades and reassured him that the mission was accomplished successfully thanks to their help.

They received their seats on the Nepalese Airline plane without any trouble and in two hours they touched down in Kathmandu.

Lobsang phoned Kathmandu as soon as the they left Lhasa and signalled to Shrestna that they were on their way. Shrestna sent the hotel bus to the airport to pick up the little group and take them to the hotel. The travellers were tired from all the excitement of the last day and retired soon to their rooms. Mrs Bolger was accommodated with Hannah.

The next morning, after breakfast, the group had a meeting. It took some time to explain to the unsuspecting Mrs Bolger that all the adventures of the last weeks were connected with the Crystal Skull about which she knew nothing.

Harvey explained how they acquired the Crystal Skull to free the Princess locked inside by the Shamans and when they tricked the Shaman by not giving him the Skull as they agreed after the Shaman freed the Princess, the Shamans kidnapped Mrs Bolger in revenge to force them to deliver the Crystal Skull in exchange to Mrs Bolger.

At Mr Harvey's suggestion they wanted to put questions to the Skull about what they should do next now that the Princess was freed and Mrs Bolger was rescued, seeing that they had managed to keep the Skull safe from the Shamans so far.

"Before we turn to the Skull I wish to remind you that our life was interrupted by accepting the Princess' request to free her and that as you kids are only at the beginning of your life and your career, you should finish your schooling first of all."

"Here, here," joined in Mrs Bolger.

"Have you thought about your immediate and about your more distant future?"

"I will definitely go to college after matriculating and wish to become a history teacher, like you, Dad," answered Hannah. Matthew said the same.

"Well then, now we have to find out what 'our friend', if I may address it so, has in mind." With this Harvey took out the Skull from the box and placed it on the table. Before touching the cranium part, he signalled Mrs Bolger to keep quiet. This was her first experience with the Skull.

"What do you suggest we should do to disengage our mundane life from yours to be safe from those who have plans, maybe grandiose plans, involving you and what should we do to secure your safety?"

Hannah and Matthew knew better than expecting the Skull to make an audible answer but Mrs Bolger looked right and left not knowing what to expect.

Finally Harvey explained to Matthew's Mom that he had received the answer telepathically. "The Skull wishes us to place it in a secure legal custody, perhaps in the Smithsonian Institute in Washington. They'd be able to provide a story to cover our and of the Skull's absence from public view for the last week."

They all agreed that they should return to Chicago as soon as possible and there Mr Harvey should use the first two days to make the arrangements with the Smithsonian people.

Back in Chicago, Mrs Bolger reported to her boss that she had had an accident that kept her away from work and promised to show up in two or three days.

Mr Harvey phoned his Principal at Chicago-South high school. He told him that he was suddenly, unexpectedly detained after work and employed on a confidential government research project with the condition that nobody should know about his whereabouts. "I will be free within a couple of days," he promised.

He then phoned the Director of Acquisitions of the Smithsonian Institute and told him that he wished to donate a rare, priceless object to the Institute but he couldn't leave Chicago nor trust the object to the Post Office. He suggested the Smithsonian should send a responsible person with an armoured car to him and collect the object.

After checking Bert Harvey's identity and calling him back, the offer was accepted and the following day an employee of the Smithsonian arrived in an armoured car. Mr Harvey told him that his name and the circumstances of how the Institute received the Crystal Skull should be kept confidential. Furthermore, he asked that the Smithsonian send him a certificate that he had been detained on confidential government business.

Two days later a report was published in the Chicago Tribune about the hijacking of an armoured car on the Chicago-Washington Highway. Two bodies were found by the Police in the burnt out car. One was the driver. The Police are investigating the identity of the other body and the contents of the car. They suspect it was an insider job.

Mr Harvey told Hannah and Matthew that he would not contact the Smithsonian to find out what they knew about the whereabouts of the Crystal Skull. "It is better if our lives are not connected anymore with that of the Skull's," he said, then added, "I can't help feeling, though, that we will still hear from it, but we should now concentrate on leading our lives as we planned."

After matriculation Hannah and Matthew entered different colleges and they had only occasional meetings at youth organizations.

PART II

CHAPTER FIFTEEN

AFTER MATTHEW'S MOTHER WAS FREED from the Shamans' captivity in Lhasa, Hannah, Matthew and Harvey returned to Chicago. Hannah and Matthew received extension from the school and finished their graduation exams successfully. Professor Harvey asked for a fortnight's holiday to visit his old friends at the Waterloo University in Canada. He wanted to thank them for their help in the adventure they had had with the Crystal Skull in Tibet.

"We couldn't have freed Matthew's mother from the Shamans without the help of your comrades," Harvey told Evan Godfrey, and thanked him again for everything.

He also thanked the Vice Chancellor, Benjamin Ottamar, for the covering letter stating that the Harveys were on an 'official research trip'. "It gave us a feeling of security in case the Chinese became suspicious and hostile."

One evening, Dr Godfrey invited Harvey for a 'family dinner'. To Bert's surprise, Mrs Godfrey was not present but there was a pretty girl about the same age as his daughter, Hannah.

"I didn't know you had a daughter, Evan," Bert remarked. "Isn't Mrs Godfrey eating with us?"

He only saw then that Evan was tense, nervous.

"You didn't know my big daughter, Dawn. She was away in France, where she finished her high school studies. Her mother is in Montreal right now visiting her family. I expect her to call tonight. By the way, Dawn is about to enrol in College.

When Evan stopped for a moment to clear his throat, Bert cut in, "I suppose Dawn is planning to enrol here at your university after being away that long? Hannah would be happy to enrol here too. You two would make good friends, Dawn, I'm sure."

Dawn smiled, contemplating her answer. She didn't say a word, just watched for her father's reaction. But he seemed distracted.

"You'll have to forgive me for a moment. I'll ring my wife. She should have phoned hours ago. I hope there is nothing wrong. I won't be long." With this he left the room.

Bert Harvey and Dawn had difficulty finding anything to speak about while waiting for her father to return.

"Are you happy to be back at home, at Waterloo, with your parents and with your old friends?" asked Bert finally. Before Dawn could answer, her Dad returned. He was obviously upset.

"Is Mom all right?" asked Dawn.

"I hope so. I don't know. She hasn't arrived yet. Didn't phone, either. I tried to call her on her cell phone too, but she didn't answer."

"Do you have any particular reason to worry about her?" asked Bert.

"Unfortunately, I do. The day before she left I had a phone call from Lhasa. They told me that two Tibetan comrades who helped you there have disappeared. The following day their bodies were found at the bottom of a gorge. Both were Waterloo graduates."

"Do you think they were kidnapped, and talked?"

"There is no way they talked. I know them. But what if we have a traitor in the organization?"

"Do you think they would seek revenge for freeing Mrs Bolger without giving them the Skull? Or would they try to scare you off from further interference?"

The two men fell silent, deep in thought.

"What is happening with Mom? What organization are you talking about?" demanded Dawn.

The two men looked at each other, their faces mirroring uncertainty. Dawn looked at them with expectation, then growing impatience. "Do you want to keep something secret from me, Dad? If it's about Mom I have a right to know."

"You shouldn't think that, darling. I know you are an adult and I treat you accordingly. You have every right to know what's happening in connection with your mother. The fact is, I don't know yet. And I don't know yet what we should do about it." He looked at Bert when he said 'we' and his friend nodded that he agreed, and that he could be counted on.

"First we have to find out what exactly did happen," said Bert. "It's natural to suspect that Shamans murdered the couriers of the Smithsonian Institute on their way to Washington carrying the Crystal Skull after we tricked them and freed Mrs Bolger, but why would they then kidnap your wife, if they already had the Skull? Could there have been two different gangs? But who could they be? Perhaps we should look for two gangs, one criminal gang and another one connected to the Shamans? What do you think Evan?"

"I agree. You see, Dawn darling, as impatient and desperate as we are to solve the mystery of what and why happened to your beloved mother, first we'll have to investigate the circumstances of the Crystal Skull robbery. Then we'll have to find out the connections, the possible connection, to your mother's kidnapping.

"Was Mrs Bolger kidnapped? Why?"

"You see, Darling, Bert Harvey, my old friend, took away the Skull and took it to Peru with his daughter Hannah and their friend, Matthew, to free an Inca Princess locked in the Skull by Shamans 400 years ago. They managed to free the Princess without giving the Skull to the Shamans as they agreed. In revenge the Shamans kidnapped Matthew Bolger's mother.

"Our first step has to be going to the Smithsonian Institute in Washington and digging through all documents relating to the armoured car robbery. Would you agree Bert?"

"Absolutely," he answered. "Without wasting any more time we should make an appointment with the Head of the Anthropology Department of the Smithsonian where I sent the Skull. I think his name was Huber. I'll phone him tomorrow morning. I suppose you can put me up for the night, Evan?"

"Sure I can, but let's not forget to make arrangements for our girls. Dawn could stay with her Auntie Elizabeth here in Waterloo. What about Hannah, your big girl?"

Before Bert could answer, Dawn cut in. "Really Dad. Don't you think I could take care of myself alone for a few days in my own home? How long do you plan to be away? I'll be seventeen next birthday. Mom was seventeen when you two first met. Remember?"

"It is not a matter of whether I trust you or not. Unforseen accidents could happen. I'd have no peace if I wasn't sure that you are alright. Your Auntie Elizabeth is always complaining that you never visit her. This will be a good way to make everybody happy. Be a good girl, it won't be more than two or three days."

Bert was on the point of suggesting that Hannah could come to Waterloo to keep Dawn company, but changed his mind after witnessing Dawn's reaction. After all, Hannah also had an aunt to stay with in Chicago.

CHAPTER SIXTEEN

THEY HAD A WALK AFTER dinner in the cool park of the university then Bert phoned Mr Huber in Washington at the Smithsonian Institution. Huber remembered that it was Bert Harvey who had donated the ill-fated Crystal Skull to the Institute.

In the morning, the two professors packed their briefcases with changes of underwear, laptop computers and notebooks and after the long drive they arrived that same afternoon at the Smithsonian Institute in Washington. The receptionist connected them to Mr Huber, who told them that Mr Bourke in the Investigations group of the Anthropology Department was expecting them.

It was almost five o'clock when they were ushered into the office of Mr Bourke. They told him that they wished to look through all documents and photos produced in connection with the armoured car robbery on the Chicago-Washington highway, where two people were killed and the contents of the safes were stolen.

Harvey and Godfrey expected Bourke to ask a lot of questions about the purpose of their requests but Bourke asked no questions. Instead he pointed out that it was close to closing time and offered to make an office available to them for as long as they needed it and offered to keep back one of his clerks to prepare all requested materials for them to look at next morning and would be at their service as long as they require.

"You obviously must be tired by now. Tomorrow morning you could start fresh and rested."

They readily agreed, thanked Bourke for his cooperation and left to find a hotel room for a few days.

After they had a light supper in the Hibernian Hotel they retired to their rooms and had a long sleep.

In the morning they were given name-tags at the reception in the Smithsonian and were shown the room prepared for them to work in. A young man, aged 20-something introduced himself as Noel Hodge and showed them the material collected in connection with the armoured car highway robbery.

The two men already knew from the newspapers that there were two charred bodies in the car. Now they learned that the victims were the driver and the official sent from the Smithsonian to pick up the Skull. They also learned that the robbers used exploding bolts to remove the small built-in safe which contained the Skull. But who were they?

"They were two people dressed in ski outfits including masks that completely covered their heads," Hodge told them.

"Wasn't any identifying sign left?" asked Bert.

"No, nothing I know of. You could see it for yourself on the in-car video. Would you like me to show it to you?"

"There was an in-car video and it survived the fire? Sure we want to see it," said Evan who became quite excited about the possibility of getting new data this way.

Hodge put the tape into a projector and the robbery scene rolled on in front of their eyes.

First only the faces of the driver and his passenger were shown. There was no sound recording on the tape. Then the car stopped. The tape showed the surprised, perhaps frightened faces of the two men, then the car rocked violently.

"Maybe the back-door of the car was dynamited," offered Bert.

Two black-clad figures climbed into the car. They trained hand guns on the two men. They tied up the driver and the passenger, quickly stuck wide tape over their mouths and pushed them roughly to the cabin floor.

One of the figures placed explosive bolts at the points where a small built-in safe was connected to the cabin wall, separating the driver's compartment from the main cabin. Small explosions detached the safe. They picked it up without further ado.

The two figures seemed to have a short discussion before they lighted a small torch, threw it to the floor then leapt out of the car. After that only smoke was seen inside the car.

"How come the tape was not destroyed in the fire?" asked Evan.

"The tapes are kept in fire-proof casings," the clerk told them.

"Have you seen anything worthwhile, anything that could give us a clue as to the identity of the robbers?" asked Evan.

"No, not really," said Bert, "but something looked funny to me. Could we run the tape again, Noel? Watch the movements, the gestures closely. Something looked unusual to me. Let's just see the tape again."

When the tape reached the point where the two dark figures entered the car, Harvey asked Hodge to slow down the tape. "Watch the figures, watch the movements, Evan," called out Harvey. "Can't you see anything unusual?"

"Not really, sorry. What caught your attention?"

"Have you ever seen male skiers wearing pink snow glasses? Can't you see a corner of a pink shawl showing between the neck of the rubberized suit and the ski mask? And the movements? The almost cat-like, prancing movements? These two were women! It never occurred to us that the robbers may have been women. This is a whole new ball-game!"

"What difference does it make if the robbers were women? Do you think that maybe a gang of female criminals decided to rob the armoured car, knowing nothing of the Skull it carried? Do you think they were after money that armoured cars usually deliver?"

"We are not getting any closer to my wife's whereabouts," said Evan desperately. "I don't think they were criminals after money in the armoured car."

"Let's have a look at the tape again, slowly. Watch how purposefully they were acting. They didn't look around, they didn't look for money in the other locked drawers which they could have blown open the same way as the locker that had the Skull. Look, they went straight for the Skull's safe and as soon as they had it in their hands, they left. I have no doubts that they were after the Skull."

"I can see your point, Bert . Unfortunately this new element does not get us closer to finding out what happened to Patricia. Do you think this Skull robbery had nothing to do with Patricia's disappearance? I'll phone home and check if Dawn has learned anything about her mother in the meantime. Maybe she had an accident and was taken into a hospital unconscious. As bad as that would be, it wouldn't be the worst possible solution. Finding out if women robbed the armoured car is not making our investigation easier. What do you think, Bert?"

"Make the phone calls by all means, however, even if nothing new came up about Patricia, we have to continue our investigation. If the robbers were women, that doesn't prove that they were not Shamans.

"We have actually met a female Shaman, a Shura, in Machu Pichu four years ago. Do you know a channeler we could ask for help?"

"There is Abha Chetan, back in Waterloo. He is a Tibetan who used to teach at the Waterloo University after you left. He retired years ago but is living in Waterloo and I'm sure he'd be willing to help."

"Good. Let's move back to Waterloo and contact that Tibetan."

Harvey asked Hodge to make a copy of the tape they saw and of the closing report of the investigation into the armoured car robbery.

Before they left Washington, they reported to the Director that their examination of the documents did not turn up anything new, thanked him for the cooperation and left.

CHAPTER SEVENTEEN

DAWN WAS HAPPY TO GREET her returning father. She reported that there was no communication with her mother or with anybody else unexpected. Bert moved in to the Godfreys'.

Abha Chetan lived in one of the Waterloo suburbs, in a small weatherboard house. Green leafy vines covered the front of the house. There was no furniture in the room they entered. Abha was sitting on a thick, richly decorated carpet in the small front room. Candles provided the lighting. The only window was covered by the vines outside.

Abha received the visitors with a friendly smile on his brown, weather-beaten face and offered them tea. They sat opposite him on the carpet.

Evan Godfrey told him that his wife has been kidnapped, and that they, he and Bert Harvey, suspected Shamans were involved in the kidnapping and that it may have been connected to the highway robbery of the armoured car by Shamans who stole the Crystal Skull the car was carrying.

"Can you help us?" he asked.

Abha turned around and picked up a pink quartz Skull, maybe half the size of an average human skull. It had been resting in the lap of the bronzed sitting Buddha statue behind his back. Abha caressed the cranium part of the skull and murmured a mantra several times, then fell quiet while kept caressing the skull with half-opened eyes and a serene face. The visitors quietly, respectfully waited until he opened his eyes fully, replaced the skull, turned to them and spoke.

"It appears that you were at cross purposes with more than one extra-terrestrial race, while you assumed that they were from one and the same race. Even from the Orion Constellation, more then one race has visited and are still visiting Earth and interfering in earthly matters. One race is from the Rigel Star System in the Orion Constellation, and there are other Beings also from Orion. They are connected on Earth with the Illuminati, the ancient secret brotherhood. The latest frequent visitors, I call them Changelings, have been manipulating things on Earth for thousands of years. The Changelings are masters of Black Magic and mind-control. They have been trying to establish complete control over the Earth for eons.

"There have been numerous attacks against the Earth by races from the Orion Constellation in the past. At least six races from Orion took part in them but luckily for Earth, Beings from other races, namely from Andromeda and the Pleiades beat them back. Of course they were all after the same prize, total control over the Earth.

"To your question, as to wether your robbers were male or female Shamans, the answer is, the robbers of the Skull were female Shamans from Andromeda.

"Of course this does not explain what particular reason they may have had 'if' the Shamans who robbed the armoured car were the same ones who kidnapped Mrs Godfrey.

"Leave this with me and come again tomorrow. I'll meditate on this."

CHAPTER EIGHTEEN

AT HOME, A STRANGELY ACCENTED message waited for Evan Godfrey on his phone Message Bank:

"We have her," stated the male voice. "Get the *'object'* from the South and bring it to us in the North. We can exchange it for *'her'*."

That was it. It seemed obvious to the two men that the object referred to was the Crystal Skull and the 'female' person had to be Mrs Godfrey. But who sent the message? What did he mean by 'get the object from the 'South?' And where in the 'North' did he want them to take the object?

"From the 'South', where? To the 'North', where?" burst out Evan bitterly. "They speak to us, as if we had extra-terrestrial powers ourselves, like them."

In keeping with their promise to Dawn, who arrived home after her father, they allowed her to stay in the room while the discussion took place.

"Was Abha of any help, Dad?" Dawn asked.

"He is meditating over the matter. We'll see him again tomorrow. This message is a new development. I can hardly wait to see him again," her father said and wiped his forehead with his handkerchief. "It's no use to speculate and make some sort of decision ourselves. We haven't got enough information at hand. Let's eat something and then go for a walk to clear our heads."

At the next meeting, after Evan told him about the mysterious message, Abha was able to give more information.

"Shamanism is the oldest religion in Korea. It dates back to prehistoric times. In Shamanism, spirits and ghosts rule different quarters of heaven. Gods inhabit mountains, caves, trees, households. Ghosts of persons who met violent or tragic ends may also influence or change the lives of the living.

"Juju Island is the centre of Shamanism in South Korea. The Shamans who live there are mostly women. This points to the possibility that the robbers of the armoured car were females indeed and also points to Juju Island as the place which the mysterious caller referred to as the 'South'.

"The Korean female Shamans regularly practice medicine by manipulating the spirits to achieve human ends. There is no notion of salvation, moral or spiritual perfection for the believers in the spirits. The Shamans are 'professionals' who are consulted whenever the need is felt. The female Shamans of Juju Island have connection with the Andromeda Constellation since the beginning of time," concluded Abha.

"Juju Island is a large island. We have no information where on the island they could be or where are they hiding the Crystal Skull. How could we get it from them? Why would the Shamans from Orion need us, human beings, to get something for them from the Andromedan Shamans?" Bert wondered out loud.

"The reason could be that the Orion Shamans don't want to start an all-out war with the Andromedans, over getting the Skull. It may seem easier for them to use you, who obtained the Skull once already," said Abha, then added, "I'm sure you will still have more communication with the Shamans yet. The picture will get clearer then. Just be patient."

"We not only have to find the Skull on Juju Island in South Korea. Even if and when we do, and I hope to God that we will, we'll have the nearly impossible task of finding my wife in the North," complained Evan.

"Leave this with me," said Abha, "I have to approach my guardian again to ask for his help in finding the place where in North Korea the Orion Shamans are keeping her."

CHAPTER NINETEEN

THE NEXT TWO DAYS WERE busy. The two men made inquiries into which airlines would take them from Canada to Seoul. They finally agreed that Korea Air had the flights from Toronto to Seoul that suited them best.

They booked hotel accommodation in Seoul on-line, in the centrally located Cho Sun hotel. Harvey suggested they make the arrangements for going from Seoul to Juju Island when they get to Seoul. They hoped to get information about this from Abha.

Bert phoned Hannah in Chicago and told her that his leave would probably last for another week. If it took more, he'd phone Hannah again. She assured him that at home everything was alright, she had no problems and gave him her aunt's greetings.

Abha received them with the good news that he had found out where the Orion Shamans' headquarters were in North Korea.

"The Shamans are in the Songam Caves, in North Korea, in South Pyongan Province. There are 17 large caves in the natural cave-system. In many of the caves there is lighting and air-conditioning and they are open to tourists, but not all of them. One of the large caves, called 'Earthly Paradise' by the locals, for its beautiful stalactite and stalagmite formation, is blocked off by fallen rocks dislodged by an earthquake. That is where the Shamans congregate. It is likely they have Mrs Godfrey there, separated from the outside world."

Abha suggested that when they arrive in Seoul they should book into the Seoul Plaza Hotel, where many American tourists stay and they would be less conspicuous than elsewhere.

In Jeju-do (Cheju Island) they should book into the Ramadan Peace Hotel on the seashore in Seogwipo-si City on the South-Western side and not in a hotel in Jeju City on the Northern side of the island.

"In Seogwipo-si the Chief of Police is See Tae Min, a channeler, who keeps contact with me," Abha said. "He will help you. He has good contacts over the border with a few North Korean policemen. Let me see, what else," Abha stopped and closed his eyes.

"A woman who could be made up to resemble Mrs Godfrey could help a lot, both in getting the Skull from the female Shamans in the South and in getting Mrs Godfrey out of the North.

"Of course, the role of the woman should be prepared from the beginning: buying airline tickets for her as Mrs Godfrey, getting a visa into Korea for her as Mrs Godfrey. Maybe you know a Canadian Customs Officer who could help? Any ideas? Think about it," said Abha.

Leaving Abha, the two men were deep in thought. "In Jeju Island we will have to hire a car with GPS navigational map," remarked Evan, to which, as if coming out of a dream, Bert said, "What about Dawn? Couldn't she be made up to look like her mother? Clothes, hat, hairdo, spectacles, make—up, what do you think, Evan?"

"I couldn't risk Dawn. You can't be serious?"

"Of course we wouldn't put her at risk. We would be there to protect her all the time. Let's talk to Dawn and hear what she says." With this they went home to talk to her.

Dawn was waiting for them. "What did Abha say, Dad?"

"Sit down dear, I'll tell you the details."

Bert, seeing his friend hesitating and having difficulties telling Dawn that she may have to participate actively in her mother's rescue, interrupted. "Abha said that a woman made up to look like your mother could have an important part in her rescue. We'd like to know what do you think? Could you play the part of your mother?"

"It wouldn't be fair! I really don't want to risk my only daughter."

Dawn saw tears in her father's eyes, and went to him and kissed him. Then she sighed deeply. "Look at this objectively, Dad. I'm the same heights as Mom is. I have the same coloured hair. In her clothes, wearing specs and her hat, using make-up the way she did, which incidentally I've tried before, as all the girls do, I could easily pass for Mom. I want to help. I couldn't just sit at home, torturing myself knowing that you and Mr Harvey maybe are risking your lives to rescue her. You must let me go, Dad!" she pleaded, swallowing her tears.

"We'll sleep on this and discuss it tomorrow - less emotionally. I love you dear. You are a treasure," he said, holding her to him.

The next morning, with heavy heart, Evan agreed to take Dawn with him and Bert Harvey to Korea, to free her mother.

"Help me find your mother's passport dear," Evan called out to Dawn. "You are still on my passport as a juvenile but we'll have to get Korean visas for us, for Mr Harvey and for your mother too. I will buy airline tickets for all of us and the airline will arrange the Korean visas."

Godfrey phoned one of his former students from the University, Henry Dupre, who happened to be the head of the Customs Office at the airport.

In Dupre's office Godfrey told him that his wife was kidnapped a few days ago and a private agency found out that she was held in

South Korea. He had decided not to turn to the Canadian Police because the private agency seemed

confident they could rescue her and they asked not to involve the Canadian police. They would be certain to contact the Korean Police and that could jeopardise their plans, they said at the agency.

CHAPTER TWENTY

THE LITTLE GROUP DROVE FROM Waterloo to the Toronto airport with Dawn dressed up and made up to look her mother. Dupre waited for them at Passport Control and flagged through the three people with four Visas, while for the benefit of the other Customs officers, Evan Godfrey said loudly that his daughter had to visit the toilet.

They had comfortable seats on the Korean Air jumbo jet for the 12 hour flight and arrived actually 'three hours earlier' at Seoul on account of the 15 hours time difference.

During the long flight Dawn was reading the printed travel brochure and told the men some information that was new to them.

"Vaccinations are not required but are advisable particularly if travelling through cholera or yellow fever areas."

"This should not concern us," Bert Harvey reacted.

Dawn continued: "The currency is Won. One Canadian Dollar is worth 637 Won. Distance from Kimpo International Airport to downtown Seoul is 18 km. Car hiring and private driving are not recommended but there are taxis, buses and subway available. There are also numerous domestic flights."

"That's what we'll need to get off the mainland and fly to Seogwipo-si city on Jeju Island," remarked her Dad. "Is there anything else interesting darling?"

"There are other things about social customs too, though I don't know if they will concern us. Listen to these:

*learn to accept 'maybe' as an answer; understand that 'yes' can mean 'maybe', too.

*Remove shoes when entering homes and any room with tatami mats. Use both hands for handshake: use of one hand is considered disrespectful.

"I didn't know that," remarked Bert and returned to reading his travel magazine.

The food served on the plane was excellent. They could choose from a menu. They could also choose between various channels to listen to their favourite music. The Korean film screened was strange and they soon switched off their screens, closed their eyes and slept during the rest of the flight, dreaming about the adventures waiting for them.

Arrival and departure from the plane was uneventful. It was still early afternoon. "What about stamping Mother's passport with the Korean visa?' asked Dawn.

"What about it?" asked her father. "You will go through as Mrs Godfrey, with her passport. You have to get used to this, dear."

"Do we really need to stay in Seoul? We could make the Domestic Airline booking to Jeju Island from here, staying in transit. And judging by the great passenger traffic we could probably make the hotel booking on Jeju Island here too. Look, there are the counters for Domestic Airline bookings and for international hotel bookings. I bet they would accept bookings to Jeju Island too," said Dawn, as she looked proudly at the two men.

After waiting in a short queue, among mainly holidaying Koreans, they bought airline tickets for a flight connecting to Jeju-do. In another half an hour they were booked into the Ramadan Peace Hotel on Jeju-do and their plane was leaving in twenty minutes.

The flight took one hour from Seoul to Seogwipo-si on the southern side of the island. The plane flying from Seoul had to clear the 2000 metre high Hallasan Mountain crossing the island.

CHAPTER TWENTY-ONE

THE AIRPORT WAS CLOSE TO the hotel so The taxi ride didn't take more than twenty minutes. When they settled in their rooms on the tenth floor, it was still dusk and they could see from their balconies the beautiful seaside, the beaches and the green forests extending down to the sea.

After sundown they went down to the large, beautifully decorated inner court. There were small parks with flowering vegetation and small brooks with Japanese- style arched bridges. Modern, French and Japanese fashion boutiques and various international restaurants with terraces surrounded the glass covered park. At Dawn's request, they chose an Italian restaurant where they could select dishes from a menu written in Italian, English and Korean.

Dawn's attention was caught by a large mural covering one section of the wall. The mural depicted a seashore scene with birds and a stocky woman in a strange, dark, off-the-shoulder shirt standing in what seemed to be flippers, carrying a sack on one shoulder. She looked like she was wearing a crown but it was a water-proof visor, the type used by scuba divers. Her face was unmistakably Korean.

"Dad, Mr Harvey, who is that woman? What is she supposed to be doing?"

"This is your chance to learn something about Korea. Something unique," said Bert Harvey. "Well, maybe the Japanese female pearl-divers could be compared to them.

"That woman in the picture is a 'haenyo'. The haenyos dive several times every month when the tides are favourable, to collect abalone, octopi, shellfish and seaweed. The most interesting part is that men are not allowed to dive, due to the taxation laws on male labour. This is a historical difference between the island and the mainland. It defines the difference in the women's role. Here, the women are the bread-winners.

"In the whole of Asia, this may be the only place where the birth of a girl is celebrated more than the birth of a boy." Harvey was happy to share his knowledge.

"We'd better go up to our room," warned Godfrey. "See Tae Min is bound to show up."

Up in their room they switched on the television and were watching Korean sports news when after about twenty minutes See Tae Min knocked on the door. The middle-aged Korean man introduced himself and asked what their plans were.

For a moment there was confused silence. The men waited for each other to begin speaking, when finally Evan Godfrey spoke up. "We don't know how much Abha told you. We came to seize the Crystal Skull from the female Shamans in this area and deliver it to the North in exchange for my wife. She was kidnapped and taken by the Shamans to the North. Of course, we wouldn't have dreamt of initiating this action without Abha's promise that you would help us."

"I will help you, but first I have to make some inquiries. I will see you tomorrow evening here to discuss the plan of action," said See Tae Min and left.

The next day they went down the seashore where they heard the sound of strange cries echoing from the seaside cliffs. A well-known phenomenon of the place.

There was a life-size statue of a haenyo woman on the nearby Jungmun Beach. "It is commemorating the bravery of the haenyo women, who are diving sometimes so deep that they are risking their lives," explained Bert.

They saw stocky female divers totter in flippers toward the decorated sea wall and the cavernous openings behind the steps leading into the sea, where they plunged into the ice-blue water. They submerged without scuba tanks.

A young woman tending a flower stand greeted them with a friendly smile. Bert returned the greeting and a short conversation started with the girl who spoke English. They learned a lot about the haenyos from the girl.

"There used to be 30,000 haenyo divers here before the war. Now there are maybe 6,000 and half of them are about sixty years old. According to government regulation only divers' daughters can officially inherit the lifestyle. Diving is considered taboo for men. My mother is a diver too, but I'd rather search for a different role for myself," finished the friendly girl.

After five o'clock they returned to the hotel and waited for See Tae Min, who arrived an hour later. Without much ado the Korean told them about his plan.

"Your daughter," he said, pointing at Dawn, "will be used as the bait. Hang on, she will not have to face any danger," he said when he saw that her father wanted to interrupt him. The basic plan is to send her into the cave direct from the beach, carrying a box, acting as a tourist, asking naive questions from the women in the cave. They are of course shamans, or mudangs, as we call them here. Her questions should be about the weather, the sea, fishermen and so forth. Nothing to make the mudangs suspicious. A short while later we, the Police, will arrive and tell the mudangs that according to reports we received, a Western girl is delivering heroin into this cave in 5 kg packages every day and we have to search the cave for hidden drug stashes. Your daughter will be escorted out and one officer will report to me that traces of heroin were found in her box. After this scene we'll search the cave and we'll find the box with the Crystal Skull at the place where it was kept according to my informer. We'll take the names of all present and leave."

After listening to the Korean, Bert and Evan were impressed but wanted to ask questions about the preparations they had to do, and about their own roles in the action.

See Tae Min gave the following instructions: "The girl has to be dressed as she usually is, no make-up, and only a simple straw hat. She has to buy a box, like the one travelling ladies keep their hats in and before leaving the hotel, carrying the box, she has to go to Reception and ask something, just so that they'd see her with the box, dressed as herself.

"You men should rent an Avis car with a GPS, a satellite tracking device. You could follow the Police car at approximately 100 metres distance and wait outside while we we're in the cave. Coming out, in possession of the Skull, I will let the girl go to you but I will take the Skull with me to keep it safe. I will let you know about the details before we leave in the morning.

"Prepare yourself for tomorrow morning. Be ready at seven."

CHAPTER TWENTY-TWO

At seven o'clock See Tae Min arrived in a car, in a Police Captain's uniform and with six other policemen.

"You saw the statue of the haenyo woman close to the edge of the water," he said to Dawn. "Opposite the statue there are steps leading into the water. Behind the steps is the opening of a large cave. It seems to be uninhabited but that's where the mudongs are. Did you buy a box for the skull? You did. Okay. Take the box, show it to the Reception, go to the beach, walk down the steps and enter the large cave. If there is somebody, maybe a woman, and she asks you what are you looking for, tell her that you are a tourist and you heard there are wall paintings in that cave. Ask her where the paintings are, ask whether fishermen are using the cave. Ask her about the tide, whether the tide is entering the cave. Ask her anything, just play for time. Don't let her get rid of you. We'll be there in about twenty minutes. We will 'arrest' you and one policeman will escort you out to your father.

"You gentlemen just wait a bit away from the beach, in the car. As soon as we've got the skull, I will contact you and we'll leave for the

North-Eastern port, from where we'll leave the island immediately. The car ride will take only one hour across the island but the boat trip up north to the armistice line will take all day. It is almost 600 km.

Dawn played her role well. She was still in an argument about the wall paintings with a woman when See Tae Min and his men had arrived. They took away her box and escorted her out of the cave. The policemen questioned the woman about the alleged heroin traffic and heroin stash in the cave and started to search the cave systematically. They found the Skull in a box hidden under an altar covered with food and fruits prepared for the Gods. They took the woman's name, personal data and left.

The party in three Jeeps - See Tae Min and one officer with the driver in the first car, Evan, Dawn and Bert in the second car and four policemen in the third car - drove around Seogwipo Bay then turned on to the highway leading to Sehwa-ri Bay on the North-East shore where a military patrol boat was waiting for See Tae Min.

During the one-hour drive, the 'tourists' saw for the first time that Seogwipo Bay had a large harbour with a separate freight shipping section and a smaller port for leisure vessels and colourful tourist boats. Passing Seogwipo Bay they saw the Jongbang Waterfall which emptied direct into the sea. The road curved among the foothills of Hallasan Mountain. The landscape was fascinating. They passed forest-covered hills, valleys and craters of inactive volcanoes.

"I didn't know Korea had so many volcanoes," remarked Dawn and the men added that neither did they.

The vegetation was full of surprises. They saw strange midget palm trees, at least their trunks looked like palm trees.

They were less than one metre tall, had thick trunks and green, dense hair-like coronas. They saw crimson-coloured plump fruits, or were they flowers? They couldn't tell. They had bright green petals bursting out of the fruits.

After about one and a half hours, driving always in a North-East direction, they arrived at Sehwa-ri Bay. There See Tae Min drove straight on to the wharf and stopped the car at a plank attached to a grey military patrol boat lying at anchor. The two men were surprised. They didn't expect military involvement. After everyone had embarked, they heard the anchor-chain being pulled up and the engines starting.

See Tae Min told the group they could stay on the deck, or go down into the mess hall where they could get lunch, coffee or tea, but no alcohol.

Travelling on the fair-sized, but still not very large, patrol boat proved to be a bone-shaking and stomach-churning experience for the group who were not used to this way of travel. Time passed slowly. From time to time the sea seemed to become angry and huge waves shook the boat. *Are we going to finish up on the bottom of Korea Bay?* Wondered Evan but said nothing, so as not to scare Dawn. They dozed off for short periods but the heaving of the waves tossed the boat up and down and they woke soon. A couple of times See Tae Min visited the group in the mess hall and told them how long the journey would still take.

"He is a smart man," said Bert to Evan, after See Tae Min explained his plan for the next move. "We will arrive about 4 p.m. at the delta of the Taeng-don River. The river is the border between North and South Korea.

"There is a peninsula just north of the river delta. The demarcation line is cutting across that in an East-West direction. That is where we will anchor. A couple of kilometres to the East there is a bridge with sentries on both sides of the river.

"How will we cross the border? I heard about North Korean border guards shooting tourists who wander into their territory," said a worried Evan Godfrey.

"Stop worrying, everything is taken care of," said See Tae Min. "Through unofficial contacts I advised the Captain of the Northern District that gangsters from the North kidnapped your wife in Seogwipo-si, took her to the North and are keeping her at the Songam Cavern. I also told him that according to our information the gangsters crossed the border in this section for which he is personally responsible to prevent incursions from the North. He agreed that to avoid an international scandal and losing his position - or status - he'll cooperate to find the kidnapped American tourist and help us return with her to the South. By the way, you did bring Mrs Godfrey's passport with you, to prove that she was indeed in the South?" he asked. "Good, good. That is our proof that she was indeed in the South. You will come with us to identify your wife. Your daughter and the other gentleman will stay on this side and wait for us."

CHAPTER TWENTY-THREE

DISEMBARKATION FROM THE PATROL BOAT proceeded without a hitch. On whistle signals by the boat's Captain, two South Korean soldiers from the nearest Border Guard station – designated KPA#4 - came running.

They helped to stabilize the plank from the boat to the shore. They then escorted See Tae Min, three of his officers and the three Americans to the guard house.

The terrain along the river shore was neglected uncultivated gray land up to the bridge and further on as far as they could see. A stone-covered road crossed the bridge which came from the South. The bridge was a timber structure about 50 metres long, protected on both sides with 1.5 metre high timber hand-rails supported every 20 cm by timber uprights.

In the windows of the guard house on the other side, guards were clearly visible. There was a red and white barrier across the bridge on the Northern side. The guards on the Southern side gave flag signals which were answered immediately by the opposite side. Then they started to remove the barriers blocking cross traffic.

See Tae Min and two of his officers shed their uniforms in the guardhouse. Bert was surprised to see that the wardrobe was full of civilian clothes. *They must have used this crossing to enter the North before,* he thought. See Tae Min and the soldiers with Evan crossed the bridge in civilian clothes while one officer stayed on with Bert and Dawn. He saw that See Tae Min turned his back to the others while he changed into civilian clothes. He took the Skull out of its box, covered it with sack-cloth and put it into his backpack.

"There is nothing to be afraid of for your Dad, or for your Mom," Bert said to Dawn, "everything is well organized."

Arriving to the Northern side, Evan Godfrey was surprised to see two Jeeps ready to take them to their target. As they started off in a North-East direction on a stone covered narrow road See Tae Min explained to him that the Songam Caverns were about 10 km away in Kaech'on-si District, which belongs to the South Pyongan Province. "They are popular curiosities and you'll mingle with many tourists - Japanese, American and Koreans - but you don't have to worry about being discovered, or unmasked. My colleague is taking care of our security.

CHAPTER TWENTY-FOUR

THE TWO JEEPS, WITH THE Northern Captain and two of his soldiers in the first, See Tae Min, Evan Godfrey and See's two soldiers in the second, drove from the guard house towards the East until they reached the Songam Caves.

The road approaching the Caves got wider and groups of tourists, Japanese, Korean and a few Westerners were moving toward the Caves.

"Won't these tourists interfere with our operation?" See Tae Min asked the Captain.

"We will see that when we get there," said the Captain, unfazed.

However when they reached the entrance to the Caves they realized that they did have a problem. There was a barricade manned by soldiers and an Officer was allowing people in only after they paid for tickets.

"What now? I suppose you could get us in despite the guards but searching for the prisoner inside and getting her out will be impossible through this crowd," said See Tae Min to the Captain.

"Wait," he said in answer. He got out of the Jeep and approached the guards.

On his return he explained. "There is a Festival with sacrifices to the Gods inside. We couldn't possibly disturb it without causing a riot and the guards would obviously ask for reinforcements. We'll have to wait until the show ends and the tourists are gone. It could take two or three hours. We can wait in the house where they are selling souvenirs. At the back they are selling beer. Korean beer is good," he said.

"You don't have to worry that they could smuggle your wife out while we are waiting. First of all nobody knows why we are here and there are no back exits from the Caves. Just have a beer and relax. Time will fly." With this he led he group into the back of the roadside building.

When the tourists left and the Captain led the group into the Cave, a Korean, dressed in the garb of a priest, ran up to the Captain and told him to follow him.

The group bypassed a dozen or so caves, some of which were indeed spectacular. The caves were named after the scenes suggested by the stalactites and stalagmites: Flower Gate, Waterfall, Snowscape and so on. The electric lights switched on for the tourists were still on when they reached the large cave called Earthly Paradise. There was a sign hung on a barrier, "No entry, falling rocks". The 'priest' who until then was leading the group stood aside and motioned the Captain to enter.

The Captain pushed the barrier away and entered, followed by his two soldiers, See Tae Min, Evan Godfrey and the two civilian clad soldiers of See Tae Min.

The scene was one of chaos, created by fallen rocks and broken stalactites. After looking around in the cave the Captain discovered a slit in the rock, at the back of the cave. It was behind an altar-like structure, camouflaged by a timber cover which was painted the colour of the rocks. The 'priest', standing by now at the back of the group, motioned to the Captain that the people he was looking for were in that covered section.

The Captain approached the timber cover but before he could reach it a Korean army officer, a Major, stepped out with gun held in his hand and shouted to the Captain, "You are arrested for treason," and ordered two soldiers standing beside him to disarm the Captain and his two soldiers.

The Captain moved, apparently to follow the order, pulled out his gun from its holster, but instead of throwing the gun down, he levelled it at the Major and shot him. The Major collapsed, his soldiers stood frozen.

CHAPTER TWENTY-FIVE

THE CAPTAIN ORDERED THE SOLDIERS to drop their guns and lie on the ground, then ordered his soldiers to collect their guns and guard them.

For a moment Evan Godfrey thought that their well planned action had failed and could not see how they could proceed to free his wife. However the Captain didn't seem disheartened and carried on. He will have to come with us to the South, or they would surely execute him for killing the Major, went through Evan's mind. Looking around, he noticed that the 'priest' has disappeared.

He looked at See Tae Min, who could see the confusion on Godfrey's face and smiled at him encouragingly.

The Captain shouted at the soldiers on the ground, "You have one minute to tell me where this space between the rocks leads to and where they took the woman. I will count to three, if you don't speak, you will die, like your Major did. One…"

One of the soldiers lifted his hand. "I'll tell you," he said.

"Two Shamans were guarding the woman here. Yesterday I heard them talking. One said that Southerners want to free her, but he would contact the Major, who worked for them, and the Major would shoot you when you arrive. The space between the rocks leads through the hill. There are rice paddies on the other side down to the demilitarized zone. A country road leads between the paddies to the No.3 Tunnel. Do you know the one?"

"Go on," said the Captain.

"Please don't kill me. I can lead you to the cave near to the tunnel, where they took the woman."

"Alright, you can show us the place," he said to the trembling soldier. Allowed him to stand but ordered one of his men to tie the hands of the other soldier behind his back. "You will stay here tied up and I don't care if you rot here," he said to him. See Tae Min described the tunnel they were talking about.

"Since the armistice, North Koreans have attempted to cross the armistice line several times illegally, sometime with success. Over the years, four tunnels have been discovered, staggered along the armistice line. The first reaction from the South was to blow up the tunnels but later they decided that the tunnels could serve some purposes for them too in the future. They left the four main tunnels open but placed guards at their entrances. The Northerners did too, without ever discussing the issue. They are talking about the No.3 tunnel, which is in this area."

Evan Godfrey realized then how much more complicated their job had become, and even after freeing his wife they will have new unforeseen problems, like getting back to the Southern side, but decided to help the leaders by not asking more questions.

Led by the Northern soldier, the Captain and his two soldiers entered the crevice in the rock followed by See Tae Min, Evan Godfrey and See Tae Min's two soldiers. Moving through the winding trail in the crevice in the dark was not easy. Though the Captain switched on his torch from time to time, members of the group occasionally fell and hurt themselves on the uneven rocky floor.

After struggling through the narrow crevice for about twenty minutes, the group emerged between young trees on the hill, almost level with the rice paddies which stretched far into the distance. The full Moon helped the group to proceed along the narrow country road among the rice paddies. The soldier acting as a guide moved fast. "We have to walk about five or six kilometres," he said to the Captain.

After about an hour of fast walking between the moonlit rice paddies, the solder signalled 'quiet' and stopped.

CHAPTER TWENTY-SIX

AFTER CONFERRING WITH THE CAPTAIN, See Tae Min explained to Evan that they were only about 100 metres from the opening of the cave on the left side of the road.

"Trees cover the opening of the cave so we can move quite close to it without being discovered. The Captain and his soldiers will go into the cave and

I will go with them, carrying the Skull in my backpack. You will stay outside with my two soldiers.

"It is safer this way," he said. With a heavy heart, Evan agreed. He would have preferred to be among the first ones to see his wife.

"You come with me to identify the Shamans who are guarding the woman," the Captain said to the captured soldier.

The adventurers were surprised to see how big the opening of the cave was as they stepped inside. *It is a secondary limestone formation over a lava cave,* thought See Tae Min, a former geology student. There was no way to see how deep the cave extended. Across most of the opening area, the stalactites and the stalagmites left only about a one or one and a half metre high opening but at one side the vertical space was about three metres. The top was 'decorated' with a fine stalactite curtain.

The Captain, See Tae Min and the two soldiers entered. At first they could see nothing. There was complete darkness. Holding his torch as far away from his body as he could, the Captain switched it on. There were fallen rocks and broken stalactites everywhere. The Captain realized that they could see nothing without the torch. He placed the torch at the top of a rock, switched it on and left it there. *We have a maximum of thirty minutes light now,* he reminded himself ruefully.

"Have you brought the Skull with you?" The Korean shout of a Shaman reverberated and echoed throughout the cave. *I wonder if there is only one, or are there two of them?* The Captain thought.

"We have the Skull. Send the woman down so we can see her and we'll give you the Skull," answered the Captain, who concentrated on establishing where the Shaman's voice came from. It seemed to him that the voice came from a balcony 25 to 30 metres further inside the cave. He was adamant not to leave the Skull here for the Shamans, whom he detested, without first securing the release of the woman.

"I'll bring down the woman to a fair distance from you so you can see her. You leave the Skull where you are now, so that I can see it. Then as you move away, I'll bring the woman closer to the Skull and finally leave her there once I have the Skull in my hands."

The constant use of the singular pronoun convinced the Captain that he was dealing with one and not two Shamans, as first thought.

There was only a very narrow track between the rocks leading from the 'balcony' toward the Captain's position.

He whispered to his soldiers to memorize the terrain, then switched off the torch and ordered the two soldiers, both sharpshooters, to crawl up about halfway along both sides of the track and wait crouching until he switched on the torch. That would be the signal to shoot the Shaman leading the woman in the head. The Captain knew how accurate shooters his soldiers were and trusted them.

The Captain took the Skull from See Tae Min, placed it on the ground and pointed his torch at it. The Skull reflected the light so brightly that it shone to a great distance. "You've seen the Skull, now bring the woman closer so I can see her," shouted the Captain.

There was some toing and froing when the Shaman at first did not bring Mrs Godfrey up to an observable distance, until finally the Shaman shouted, "That's it! I'm not bringing her any closer."

Suddenly there was a torch light clearly showing Mrs Godfrey, her hands tied and her mouth taped, pushed by a male figure in typical Korean peasant garb, then two shots rang out and the Shaman fell down, his head bleeding profusely. The Captain ran fast to Mrs Godfrey, pointing his gun at the collapsed Shaman.

See Tae Min grabbed the Skull, put it back in his backpack and ran out to call Evan Godfrey in.

He ran in and embraced his wife. She fainted. He quickly removed the tape from her mouth and untied her hands. She could stand on her feet only with her husband supporting her. "Let's take her out into the fresh air," said See Tae Min. "We have to think through our next steps."

CHAPTER TWENTY-SEVEN

IN THE FIRST RAYS OF the sun, sitting in the mouth of the cave, the Captain spoke first.

"I will leave the North and go with you of course. There is nothing to discuss about that. I want to give a choice to my soldiers, both the ones who fought with me and those two are still guarding the tunnel; either to come with me, or get tied up so they could claim to have been overpowered. I know the routine. They would be freed by the changing guards at 8 am. "Speak up men," he said, turning to his two soldiers.

"I would like to follow you, Captain," said the older soldier, "but I have a family, children to take care of. I cannot leave them." The other soldier quietly said that he was in the same situation. They both stood there with hanging heads, their confusion was shown on their faces. They were not used to making such important decisions for themselves. They were used to doing as they were told.

The Captain suggested to See Tae Min that he use his field-phone to warn the Northern guards of the tunnel that he was coming with a group of people to inspect it. "This will be enough to ensure that they can enter the tunnel and disarm the guards," he said. "You should do the same. Contact the Southern guards and warn them that we are coming, led by you."

The Captain's plot worked. The Northern guards of the tunnel greeted them and after a few tense moments submitted to being tied up by the Captain's soldiers. They decided to stay in the North like their two comrades. Guards on the Southern side of the tunnel accepted See Tae Min's identification without any problem and followed his instructions.

The Northern guards had only one Jeep and that wasn't enough to transport eight people. See Tae Min ordered one guard at the border crossing to come with them and with the tunnel guards' Jeep, the two cars transported everybody to the anchored patrol boat. See Tae Min promised the Northern Captain that he personally would act with the authorities to get special immigration rights to the Captain in recognition for his services in freeing Mrs Godfrey.

It was already dark when after a full day sea voyage, the patrol boat with members of the group anchored at the wharf in Seogwipo Bay.

For two days the Godfrey family and Bert Harvey rested at the Ramadan Peace Hotel. Godfrey arranged for a doctor to visit Mrs Godfrey and examine her for any damage the forced kidnapping and imprisonment might have caused to her health. According to the doctor's opinion, though she was extremely exhausted she was not suffering any permanent damage. Being together with her daughter and her husband again seemed to restore her well-being.

After expressing their deep gratitude to See Tae Min for his efforts, the Godfreys invited him to visit them in Canada whenever it suited him. The four North Americans flew from Seogwipo-si to Seoul where they changed planes and flew to Toronto. In Toronto there was a teary farewell when they parted. Bert Harvey flew to

Chicago and the Godfreys to Waterloo. They promised each other they would keep closer ties in the future.

Before they parted company, however, Bert Harvey and Evan Godfrey had to decide what to do with the Crystal Skull. Bert carried the Skull until now in his backpack. They had to think hard about what to do with the thing which had caused them so much trouble. When making their decision, they had to think about much more than just how their personal lives were involved. They knew that potentially the peace of the world was at stake, and they really did not feel capable of making decisions about what would be best for the whole world.

With heavy hearts they decided that the best they could do was to secrete the Skull away where it would stay hidden and unapproachable. They of course did not have a place like that themselves. After rejecting many solutions, none of them thought suitable, they decided that best would be to place the Skull into the custody of a non-political institution with experience in guarding unique items. The only one they knew of that filled the bill was the Smithsonian Institute. They agreed that Bert, who had previous personal contact with the Director of the Smithsonian, would travel to Washington with the Skull and explain to the Director the circumstances surrounding it. He would leave the Skull at the Institute, with the agreement that there would be no public announcement about the Institute holding the Skull and they would not put it on public display in the foreseeable future.

The Director understood and agreed to the conditions. With that, and with a deep sigh on finishing the hardest quest he had had in is life, Bert Harvey returned to his native Chicago where his lovely daughter Hannah greeted him in the company of Matthew Bolger, her friend and fellow adventurer in the previous quest.

On the 15th December 2012, he attended a conference in Washington. After the conference he had another half day before his flight back to Chicago. He decided to visit the Director of the Smithsonian Institute, where his reception was friendly. After discussing the capricious Washington weather and the latest Presidential campaign, Bert Harvey asked, if there was any problem with the Skull?

"None at all," answered the Director and offered him a chance to see his 'baby', to see personally that it was being well cared for. He phoned his Chief of Security and asked him to bring him the Skull without mentioning anything about it to other employees.

Bert Harvey and the Director continued their chit-chat for another ten minutes. By then it seemed to the Director that the Skull should have arrived from the nearby vault. He rang the Security Chief again. There was no answer. Suddenly a shrill alarm sounded.

"It is a security alert," cried the Director. "All gates are closed and everybody leaving the building will be searched. All premises will be searched by specially trained employees. The alarm must have been switched on by the Security Chief. I hope it has nothing to do with Skull!"

Within minutes the Security Chief reported to the Director that the Crystal Skull had disappeared from the vault. "It's unbelievable," burst out the Director. "Would you have any idea what might have happened?" he asked Bert, who had a feeling of déjà vu. The Skull has disappeared again! He hoped to God that his time it didn't involve him and his loved ones.

"I have a warning for you, Mr Director. Today is the 16th December 2012. In five days it will be the 21st December. This is the date that was prophesized by the Mayans to be 'the end of the world' and the Crystal Skull is supposed to have a central role in that. You have to keep the disappearance of the Skull an absolute secret to avoid a possible world-wide panic. I'm leaving. There is nothing I can do to help you to recover the Skull."

With that, Harvey left and flew back to Chicago. Using words that he hoped could not be understood by anyone else, he warned his friend Evan about the disappearance of the Skull. They agreed there was nothing else for them to do but wait and hope.

About the Author.

Tibor Timothy Vajda was born in Budapest, Hungary. He emigrated with his family to Australia in 1956, and settled in Sydney. Vajda was registered and practiced as a Surgeon Dentist from 1962-1993. After an internationally successful clinical and academic career in Oral Implantology and Biomedical Engineering he turned to full-time writing.

In his writing Vajda uses the information he absorbed in his Psychology, History, Geography and Politics studies in five languages during his frequent round the world trips.

By 2008 Vajda published nine books and more than two dozens short stories in Australia and the United States. He has received several Awards in Short Story Competitions.